THE
MARRIAGE OF
INCONVENIENCE

THE MARRIAGE OF INCONVENIENCE

BY

NINA SINGH

First published in Great Britain 2017
By Mills & Boon, an imprint of HarperCollins*Publishers*
1 London Bridge Street, London, SE1 9GF

Large Print edition 2017

© 2017 Nilay Nina Singh

ISBN: 978-0-263-07163-4

MIX
Paper from
responsible sources
FSC
www.fsc.org   **FSC® C007454**

Printed and bound in Great Britain
by CPI Group (UK) Ltd, Croydon, CR0 4YY

For my generous, kind-hearted,
and encouraging husband.
And for my amazing, wonderful children,
who make me proud every day.

Also Barb, Dee and Deb.
You've been there every step of the way
and I am thankful beyond words.

CHAPTER ONE

So now she needed his help.

R. J. Davet shifted in his chair and looked down for the third time at the email message waiting for him on his laptop. Even if she hadn't signed the message, he would have known whom it was from. Brief and to the point, apologetic yet demanding at the same time. All the characteristics of the woman he had known better than anyone else on earth. He almost laughed at the thought. He had known her intimately once. And it had cost him.

Outside his hotel window, the crowded street in London's East End bustled with activity. Delivery trucks skirted around the road. Morning commuters rushed to work, and cafés were filling with caffeine-hungry customers.

A silver tea tray with steaming scones sat untouched on the antique table next to him. He was oblivious to all of it. His appointment with the investors in a few minutes, the importance of this trip, the weeks of preparation. He couldn't bring himself to think of any of that now. After all this time, and all the pretenses, she was asking for his help.

A fleeting impulse to ignore the request entered his mind. After all, she hadn't indicated it was urgent. Every self-preserving instinct told him to pretend he'd never received it.

But that thought was gone in a second. He would go to her. Of course he would. Even with the little information the message provided, he couldn't ignore a plea from her. Besides, the past was behind them now. There was no reason he couldn't assist her professionally. He was the best. Arrogance or immodesty had nothing to do with it. He knew his strengths and he knew his shortcomings. He knew his reputation within the field had compelled celebrity and politician alike to seek out his expertise, even this early in his business. He'd worked his butt off since leaving college.

Now his skills were being sought by the one woman who could have had that and a lot more at her disposal. The bitter tang of memory formed an unpleasant taste in his mouth before he swallowed it.

Rubbing his eyes, he stood and read the email once more.

R.J.

It's been a while. I find myself in the unexpected position of requiring your assistance. Only you have the background. Let's discuss at your earliest convenience.

She'd included a small icon of a dancing couple at the end: *What do you say, Princess? Shall we dance?*

He leaned forward to reply to her and stopped himself. There was no reason they couldn't interact like the true professionals they were, but there was also no reason to be hasty either. He wasn't going to jump the instant she snapped her fingers. No doubt that's what she expected. Surprise for her, he'd changed.

He powered off the laptop and packed it into his briefcase, making sure hard copies of the financial spreadsheets were there. He had a lot to do in the few short hours before his flight back to the States. He didn't need a distraction like her just now.

His estranged wife would get his answer soon enough.

"He's here, you know."

Angeline Scott jumped at the announcement,

then tried to calm herself before turning away from the window. She leveled a gaze at her assistant, who was also her dearest friend.

"He's here," Shanna repeated. "R.J. just signed in downstairs. He's on his way up."

Angeline managed a nod in acknowledgement. She couldn't go through with this.

"Shan, I think we should just forget this whole thing. I'm not even going to tell him why I asked him here. I've changed my mind."

"Are you going to ask your father, then? For the money?"

Angeline gave her friend the side eye for that question. "You know that's out of the question. I refuse."

Shanna rewarded her with a look of pride. "That would only be a temporary fix anyway."

"But to ask R.J. to do this…" Angeline let herself trail off.

"We really have no choice, do we?"

"I guess not. But I know him. He's going to look at me like I have two heads, pop a hand on his hip—" she fisted her hand and set it on her hip in demonstration. "And then he's going to laugh. Then he'll become angry because he'll think it's a joke. At his expense. That's exactly what will happen." She blew a stray strand of hair off her fore-head, then added, "Not necessarily in that order."

"Then why did you ask him in the first place?"

"Because he's the only one who really quali-fies, isn't he?"

"True. Technically he's still your husband."

Angel sighed. Yes, R.J. was still her husband. In name only. The only reason being that they had never gotten around to finalizing their divorce. And now, after close to three years apart, she had to demean herself by asking him to pretend they'd never split up at all.

Shanna smiled at her. "Go straighten yourself out, Angel. Your cheeks are flushed. It's just not becoming on someone with your olive skin tone. And those curls." She held a hand up in frustra-tion to the mass of unruly hair Angeline knew was spilling out of her loose bun. "We can do this. Just pull yourself together. It's the only way."

Angeline plunked herself into the wide leather chair behind her. Shanna was right, of course. They had gone through every other feasible option.

"Fine," she said, then looked up in defiance. "But I refuse to straighten myself out."

Shanna stole a quick glance into the outer room.

"Looks like you don't have time for it anyway. Our fella just walked in."

Angeline gripped the armrests on the chair and tried to assume a perfect poker face. Her heart was in her throat, and adrenaline coursed through her veins like a river during a storm. But she was certain none of it showed. R. J. Davet might turn her insides to lava, but she knew how to mask emotion well.

Shanna gave her a reassuring wink and went to show him in.

Angeline took advantage of the time to try to calm her nerves. She was a mature business-woman now. Not a foolish young college student. She'd graduated top of her class, even with the distraction that was R. J. Davet.

He wouldn't affect her the way he used to. She was much wiser with a good head on her shoulders. She was over her once all-consuming attraction to him. She was over *him*.

Angeline stood up to greet him, feeling much more certain of herself. It was ridiculous to think he could still hurt her.

But then he walked in. And it hurt just to look at him.

She managed to curve her lips into a smile.

"Hello, R.J. Long time, no see." She cringed as soon as she said it. Nothing like dazzling him with witty conversation.

He didn't say anything for a long moment, merely looked at her. Just for an instant, the hurt fell away and she was staring into hypnotic, deep chocolate eyes that were so familiar. There was nothing between them, there was nothing around them. As if sensing her thoughts, his expression suddenly became aloof and guarded.

"Hello, Angel." He smiled when he said it, but his eyes remained distant.

He made his way toward her with the same confident gait she remembered. Except now there was so much more polish. In a dark Italian-cut suit, he had the elusive manner that only self-made successful people have. He looked like the powerhouse he'd always wanted to be, had always talked about becoming. He looked like the man he had left her to become.

She checked the impulse to step back as he approached, afraid of her reaction. His wavy black hair reflected almost navy where the light hit it. The strong set of his jaw lent a hardened austerity to his face.

Her dreams had not done him justice.

She cleared her throat. "So, I hear your business is doing well. You're trying to expand Davet Corporate Security into Europe, aren't you?"

"That's the intent, yes." His voice rang clear with impatience.

"I can't believe all you've accomplished in the short time since college."

He gave a slight nod in her direction. "Likewise."

Angeline felt herself shiver. R.J. wasn't interested in small talk. "It must have been a surprise to hear from me after all this time," she said in a lower voice.

"Getting your message was a few notches higher than surprise. Closer to shock, actually."

She tried not to bristle at the hostility in his voice.

R.J. shoved his hands into his pants pockets. "Let's cut to the chase here, shall we? We're both busy people. You didn't call me to play catch-up. What can I do for the reigning tea queen of the Western Hemisphere? I imagine you have some type of corporate security concern. Were your systems hacked or something? Is that it?"

Regret washed through her. He was obviously not thrilled about being here. While he couldn't wait to leave, she was aching inside at seeing him again. Yep, she was a fool one hundred times over. "Not exactly. Please, have a seat." She motioned him to the red brocade chair across from her desk and waited for him to sit down.

Swallowing past the lump of apprehension in her throat, she began, "I'd like to discuss a business proposition with you. An alliance, so to speak."

She saw the curiosity flash in his eyes before he managed to suppress it. "What type of an alliance would the head of a thriving tea retail and distribution business form with the CEO of a corporate security firm?"

"I need your help. But not in the way you think."

He lifted a brow in question. "I'm listening."

Angeline walked over to the large window overlooking metro Boston. Past the traffic, the Charles River gleamed like liquid gemstone as the sun reflected off the water. Her back to him, she could feel the intensity of his gaze and imagined his eyes roaming over her. The way his hands had not so long ago. She squeezed her eyes shut.

Somehow she managed to find her voice again. "I'm in some trouble and it could affect other people. A lot of other people."

He was up and behind her in an instant. She

recognized the poignantly familiar scent. That same distinctive cologne coupled with the aroma that was purely male and purely his. She tried to still the shaking in her hands and clasped them together in front of her. Heavens, this meeting was playing havoc on her senses. Pure attraction. Attraction that in the end hadn't been enough to keep them together. But the flames of desire apparently still burned strong.

For her anyway.

"Angeline," she heard him say. "Are you in some kind of danger?"

She took a moment to answer. Technically she wasn't. But in every other sense she was. Without warning, a firm set of hands gripped her by the shoulders and turned her around.

"Answer me."

"N-no, I'm not in any danger," she managed to stutter while fighting the urge to lean into the strong, masculine chest that was so close.

He dropped his hands. Disappointment pummeled her. He clearly wasn't as interested in touching her as he had been once.

Better to get this over with. "It's the business, R.J. The TeaLC chain. I'm worried that if I don't expand soon, we may not survive."

He quirked an eyebrow. "But I thought your business was flaring."

"It's also very costly. The distribution end brings in a good amount, but the retail chains aren't terribly profitable. Plus, I have some very expensive overhead. I need a sales spurt, soon." She took a deep breath. "And I think I just may have come up with a way to achieve some growth."

"But?"

"But it won't be easy."

He narrowed his eyes. "Go on."

Here it was, the tough part. She braced herself for the certain embarrassment and decided to just blurt it out. "We never signed the papers to finalize our divorce."

A dark shadow flashed in his eyes. "Is that what all this is about? You want to take care of the divorce finally?"

"No! No, that's not it at all." This was even harder than she would have imagined. "Actually, it's kind of the exact opposite."

Silence. He searched her face for clarification.

"I need to act like I'm happily married. Just for one night. I need you to pretend we're still a fully married couple who never separated." Oh, man, she was making a complete and utter mess of this whole proposal. But there was no way to back out now.

She lifted her palms in appeal. "It wouldn't be for long. I realize what I'm asking and—"

He cut her off with a quick raise of his hand. "Let me get this straight. You have to act like you're still happily married to grow your business."

Before she could answer, he turned around and walked toward the center of the large room.

She stepped toward him, afraid he was going to leave without hearing her out. She'd gone too far to back out now. As difficult as this was, she had to see it through.

"R.J., wait. Can I just explain?"

He didn't answer. Angeline rubbed her arms to calm herself. He was so angry he couldn't even speak!

And then he turned around, looked into her eyes and broke into laughter.

She really was too much.

R.J. didn't know if he was laughing more from amusement or the unsettling experience of seeing her again. This had to be some kind of joke.

He didn't feel much like laughing, though, when

she lifted those deep brown eyes up to his. She looked like a wounded doe.

His breath caught in his throat. "Wait a minute. You're serious."

"I wouldn't have asked you to come all the way out here if I wasn't serious."

"I think I'm missing something here."

"This isn't some attempt at a reconciliation. I know things are over between us."

"You're right about that."

She flinched. "I just need you to do some convincing acting for a day or so."

"You want me to pretend we're still completely together? That I'm still your husband in every way." He'd done everything he could for the past three years to try to forget what that was like. "What kind of game are you playing?"

"It's not a game, it's a business proposition," she said in a firm, official voice.

A what? He had to try to calm down. No one else could ever get him so riled up. Taking a deep breath, he concentrated his gaze on her face.

He wouldn't have believed she could have become more attractive. The girlish, soft qualities had been replaced with the maturity of a beautiful woman. Breeding and class were etched in every inch of her. It had thrown him off so many years ago, the passion that lay beneath her proper demeanor. Just thinking about it now was throwing him off again. Three years hadn't made enough of a difference, apparently.

"Maybe we better start from the beginning."

"It shouldn't take more than a day or so of your time," she began, becoming animated.

He lifted his hand to stop her. "Before we get too far with this scheme, suppose you fill me in on the details. What happened? Last I heard, you'd grown the business tremendously since you started it." She'd done an impressive job, too. Angeline had moved quickly on the sudden popularity of tea and had become a leading distributor in no time. She was one of the youngest successful CEOs in the United States. Like him.

"It all stemmed from such a terrific idea."

Her tongue darted to lick her lips, and he lost his concentration for a moment. Her dark features were drawn tight. Slight dark circles shadowed her eyes. Even so, her regal grace never left her. It was that quality that had knocked him senseless when they'd met freshman year at university. He'd fallen hard for the contradictory mix of private school breeding and wanton boldness. Not to mention the drop-dead body that had turned his gut to fire every time he'd laid eyes on her.

"What idea?" he asked, turning back to the conversation.

"I thought there would be some opportunity for growth given the big wave in the herbal tea market. Lots of people swear by the healing benefits of some of the herbs and plants found in tisanes. I thought we'd stress that to set us apart from the competition."

"What has that got to do with being married?"

"Well, I started doing some research. It led me to a variety of plants. It's mainly grown along the Black Sea, on a small island nation called Mondolavia."

"I've heard of it."

"I traveled there with Shanna to check it out, and true enough, the stuff is invigorating. They've been drinking it in that part of the world for years. Anyone who's tried it insists it's like a magical potion. And it tastes great. Like nothing we can compare to in this hemisphere. If TeaLC was the first chain to bring it here, it would put us in a whole other category. This could be the start of a whole new product assimilation. And we'd be the one to start it all."

"So far, so good."

She nodded with excitement, clearly taken with the idea. "We were all ready to arrange for the supplier to start shipping. Even drew up a contract for exclusive distribution rights for the next several years."

"That's fantastic. I still don't see why you'd have to be married."

She shut her eyes tightly and let out a deep breath. "That area is a completely different part of the world. The plants are all grown and processed by a very traditional Mondol family. Mila and Tavov Bay have been married for decades. They're very particular about how their product is being sold and positioned. And they don't believe it's good to do business with a single woman. They'd much rather deal with a so-called stable, family operation."

Now he understood. "And you figured you had a way to accommodate them." He didn't care that his voice was thick with sarcasm. All this time had gone by without a word from her. But suddenly she was reaching out. And for what? A business deal.

She cleared her throat. "We didn't start that

way. Shanna and I initially tried to protest. But it didn't look like they were willing to hear any arguments. Then things just seemed to spiral." She leaned back on the edge of the desk. "Next thing we knew, I was talking about my 'silent partner' husband."

"I see."

"Except for the silent partner part, it's not technically a lie."

"Is that how you see it?"

"We didn't mean to be deceptive or anything. You have to believe that. I just mentioned that I had gotten married young and was about to explain that it hadn't made me a better businesswoman. But they just latched on to the married part and asked why I hadn't said so before. I just found myself not denying it."

He was having trouble coming up with an adequate response. This was the last thing he'd been expecting when he finally heard from her again.

"It started as a language issue," she continued, near to pleading. "Though they're fluent, their English is a bit broken. Then we just had to go with it." She stepped toward him and touched his arm, her eyes imploring him to understand.

"It's just that we'd gotten so far. And then it just seemed to steamroll. I found myself telling them all about your accomplishments, that you've built your own computer security services company."

Her gaze dropped to where she'd touched him, and R.J. expected to see sparks from the contact. She removed her hand and stepped back.

"And it almost worked," she added. "They said they would be glad to do business with us. But not before they came to the States to check out the operation. And to meet the husband they'd heard so much about."

He'd heard enough. For such a smart, savvy businesswoman, Angeline had somehow put herself in an utterly ridiculous position. And had managed to take him along with her. "What in heaven's name were you thinking?" Perhaps he was being a bit too forceful, but what she'd just told him was so profoundly absurd. "I've heard of adapting to the global marketplace, but what you did is borderline slapstick."

"Listen, I'm not proud of it, but I did what I thought I had to do." A hard glint appeared in her eyes.

"Why doesn't that surprise me?"

She crossed her arms in front of her chest. "That sounds like condemnation."

"More like characterization."

Her eyes narrowed on him. "I don't know what that's supposed to mean. I do know that I've done a darn good job with this company. Don't you think I should fight for it if that's what I have to do?"

He rubbed a palm over his face. She *was* a fighter. They both were. That part he understood. He'd fought hard for everything he'd wanted. Except once. But then he'd had no choice.

He took a deep breath and tried to calm down. This was getting them nowhere. "Angel, you don't need to convince me on that score. Ever since I started hearing about your success I've known this was the perfect outlet for your abilities. I just don't understand how you plan to pull this off."

"Well, it's quite simple. You just have to pose as my husband for the day or so that they're up here." She flashed him a smile that nearly crumpled his knees.

"You're the only one who's ever had any kind of practice in the role."

And practice they had. Long, steamy nights had

often turned into languid, satisfying mornings. He cursed himself as his body started to respond to the memories.

She went on. "A few weeks after they leave, I'm scheduled to go back to their orchards to sign the deal. Right before the harvest. By then they'll have realized how mutually beneficial the partnership is. And in return for your assistance, I help you expand Davet Computer Security Services to Europe. I read somewhere you were trying to find overseas clients. I present you as our security firm and help convince all our European partners to consider hiring you. And you have your expansion."

He was about to tell her his latest trip had done just that. That he'd left London just last week with a deal to become the leading provider for a major British jewelry chain. Something stopped the words from forming on his tongue. It would be the simplest way to end this nonsense idea of hers. So why didn't he just tell her she couldn't help him?

Because he couldn't deny the fact that a lot of this was indirectly his fault. Angeline's current state of financial shortage and her lack of resources were in large part due to him and their marriage.

But he just couldn't do what she was proposing. His soul would not be able to take such a pretense. He would help her, but he'd find another way.

Angel continued to smile. Man, it was hard to deny her anything when she looked at him like that. But this was too much, he just couldn't go through with something like this.

"Angel. I'm sorry. I just can't. What you're suggesting, it's just too far-fetched. Too much of a charade. Too much could go wrong."

She lifted her palms in appeal. "But—"

"Angel, no. I'm sorry."

She looked down at the floor. All the light seemed to have gone out of her. "Then I'm sorry to have wasted your time. I see now what a mistake it was to try to involve you."

R.J. cursed silently. Nothing like a good dose of guilt to start out the day. He found himself selfishly replacing it with anger. "How could you even consider it, Angel? The two of us acting like a real couple?"

She looked up, a wealth of emotion in her eyes. Anger? "R.J. This isn't about you and me."

"It isn't?"

"It's a business deal. Nothing more."

He tried not to flinch at that. "A deal where we have to pretend we're still devoted to each other and together in every sense."

"Just for one lousy night. I'm not asking for eternity."

He rubbed a hand down his face in an effort to calm down.

"Listen, I'm sorry. But it's just too ridiculous. The idea of us acting married again."

Her gaze dropped to the floor once again. "Yes, I suppose it is."

"How about we set aside some time? You, me and Shanna. We'll put our heads together and come up with a plan." Without thinking, he reached out and took her hand in his. Her skin was soft, silky. Experience reminded him she felt that way all over. He quickly let go.

Angeline sighed. "I'm afraid there's no more time for that. It took you a bit longer to get back to me than I thought."

She wasn't looking at him. He had to strain to hear her. "The supplier will be here in less than a day. If you won't do it, I'll have to come up with something else. And fast."

Like another man to play the part maybe? That

thought had his gut tightening. Of course there had to be other men in her life. She was probably just too embarrassed to approach someone she cared about with something like this. Maybe she would even rush the divorce now so that she could go to someone else with her plea.

He knew what her response to his next question was going to be before he even asked it. "Let me put some money in the company, then. Consider it an investment. Or even a loan if you'd prefer."

As he'd guessed, she started to shake her head before all the words even left his mouth. "I can't let you do that. I know you're trying to grow as well and need those funds for your own firm."

He was about to protest when she stopped him. "And anyway, that would only be a temporary fix. This deal would actually make TeaLC profitable for years to come. We'd become sole retailer in the United States for a revolutionary beverage."

She was right. No amount of money he could extend would make up for the loss of that kind of opportunity. "Angel, I'll come up with something."

Her eyes softened, but she didn't reply. Instead, she opened the door and leaned into the outside foyer. "Shanna, would you mind seeing R.J. out, please?"

Turning back to face him, she gave him a tight smile. "Thanks for coming, R.J. It was nice seeing you again. Sorry to have wasted your time." She stepped aside to let him out of her office. And out of her life once more.

CHAPTER TWO

SHANNA SEEMED TO be taking her time summoning the elevator. And R.J. wanted nothing more than to get out of the building fast. Away from the memories, away from his ex. Only she wasn't really his ex. Not yet.

"Did you grab a cup of tea on your way up?" Shanna asked while they waited.

"Uh, no." He tried to sound polite. "That looks like quite an operation you have on the first floor, though."

Shanna nodded. "It's one of our biggest cafés."

He didn't respond. His mind was still reeling. The shock of seeing Angel again after all this time—he had to get out of here and find a punching bag or a weight bench. Anything to help him vent the frustration of not being able to touch her. Or help her. He had to think, to try to come up with a different solution. One that didn't involve the disaster she was floating.

"You should stop in." Shanna interrupted his

thoughts. "The pastries are to die for. And the tea of the day is an Indian Spicy Chai that will curl your toes." She lifted a pencil to her chin and looked him over. "Then again, you might want to order something decaffeinated."

He had to laugh at her reference to his agitation. "Angel's lucky to have an assistant with such a flair for advertising. I think I will stop down for a cup."

"Great. Make sure to tip the server well. She's in a bit of dire straits."

"Yeah?" R.J. asked with mild curiosity as the elevator doors opened. He stepped aside as Shanna stepped in and then followed.

"Yes, a single mother with a toddler to support. We're one of the highest payers. But toddlers can be expensive."

"I'll tip handsomely, then."

"Good."

Shanna continued. "Our store manager has a lot on her mind, too. A young child with severe asthma. The medical insurance she gets through her job at TeaLC is absolutely crucial. Then there's Suzan. She's a college student who has to save every penny."

R.J. stilled as understanding dawned. He refused to be manipulated. "Why are you telling me all this?" he demanded, knowing it was wrong to take his agitation out on her.

Shanna whirled on him. "Because those are the kind of people who are going to be affected if this business doesn't stay profitable."

R.J. blinked at her suddenness. This was getting ridiculous. "Shanna, you know me well enough to realize I'd do anything I can to prevent that, but… But this isn't a plan, it's a fiasco. I'll find a way to help. Just not this."

Shanna actually snorted. "Shame. This deal would have been the perfect way to grow our company and secure our employees' futures. She sank her whole trust fund into this place. There's not a penny of it left. And she won't even consider going to her father."

R.J. clamped down on the anger that surged through his chest at the mention of the man who'd sired Angeline. Water under the bridge now, but it still stung. As for Shanna, he wasn't sure what to say to her.

Shanna blew out a breath. "Unlike the rest of her wealthy family, Angeline cares about giving back to the community. It's one of the major reasons she's fighting so hard to keep this place going."

He had no reason to, but he felt a sense of pride nevertheless. "How?"

"We work with the local women's shelters, try to place those ladies when an opening comes up. Single mothers, ladies trying to figure out how to stand on their own two feet. Sometimes the money we can offer isn't great, but it's better than nothing. And it gives them a chance to be productive and useful. But it's an expensive business strategy. We spend the time and money to train regardless of past experience. And turnover's higher than standard for the industry. It's the primary reason we're not as profitable as we could be. But it's worth it. Just to be able to give those women a chance to move on."

A chance to move on. Would his own childhood have turned out differently if his own family had had such a chance? If his mother had found a way to get them away from his abusive, alcoholic mess of a father?

He shook off the memories, focusing on what Shanna had just said. He'd stopped reading about Angeline and TeaLC in the business journals because it had just become too painful. Seeing her beautiful smiling face in print. So confident, so content. Content to be without him.

"I didn't know. How many TeaLC employees fall into this category?"

"About twenty to thirty percent. A few in every store in the States."

"It does sound like a costly program." Another unsettling thought occurred to him. "Have there been threats? Ex-husbands or past boyfriends?" A lot of women in shelters had to be running from abusive partners. Something he had first-hand knowledge of.

Shanna smiled. She looked pretty proud, too. "Sure there have. Angeline won't let that stop her. There's a security presence in every store, and each one is alarmed to the hilt. The public knows we won't take any chances with our employees, so nobody's tried anything."

"She's not one to back down, is she?"

"No, she's not. And you have no idea how much it took for her to ask you this."

R.J. bit out another oath. He looked up at the ceiling and exhaled slowly, wearily. So much for not being manipulated. He fished his phone out of his pocket.

"What are you doing?" Shanna asked as the elevator jolted to a stop.

He started dialing. "I have to call my secre-

tary and tell her my schedule has changed for the
next couple of days. Where's the nearest jewelry
store?"

Shanna's dark brows lifted over her piercing
blue eyes. "Why?"

"Married people wear rings."

"That feels good doesn't it, sweetie? I know it
feels good." Angeline stroked a loving hand over
the warm, eager body nestling closer to her.

"You've missed me haven't you?" Moist, soft
eyes looked back at her with enthusiasm. Here
was total acceptance, unconditional love. Right
now it was exactly what she needed.

"I saw him again today, you know," she continued.

A knowing grunt responded.

"He came back, Max. He came back and he's
going to do it." She stopped and took a deep sigh.
"I didn't want him to know about the women. He
wasn't supposed to want to do it because of them.
But he knows now, and he's going to help."

The brown eyes staring at her started to droop
with sleepiness. "Anyway, he did that thing he
always does, where he just sort of takes command and handles all the details with efficiency

and haste. He studied all the sales projections and started doing some research on Mondolavia. The whole office was eating out of his hand." She frowned. "Especially my female crew. They couldn't do enough for him.

"Still, I didn't realize how much I'd missed that. To be able to rely on someone else without worrying about appearing weak or out of control. I've always loved the take-charge quality about him. And, of course, he's still as handsome as I remember."

She stopped for a long sigh. "Oh, Max, I think I might be making a huge mistake here.

"Anyway." Angeline shifted. "He's on his way over."

Max lifted his head at the announcement.

"That's right." She looked around the plush, Eastern decor of her condo. Would he like it? She was surprised to realize that it mattered to her. A burgundy-and-black patterned Oriental rug adorned the hardwood floor. It matched the draperies that hung from the bay windows on each wall. The full-floor condominium had a large kitchen and two bedrooms positioned on opposite sides. A far cry from the one-bedroom apartment they'd shared off campus for their brief union as man and wife.

"He's bringing over some of his stuff," she continued to her captive audience of one. "We have to look like a genuine married couple."

The chime of the doorbell interrupted them. Max moved himself off the sofa and made a mad dash to the door.

"Traitor," Angeline mumbled.

On shaky legs, she went to let R.J. in. As soon as she opened the door, Max barreled into him.

R.J. laughed in surprise. Bracing himself, he looked across the threshold at her. "I can't believe he remembers me."

She smiled. Max had been the poor soul to hear all about her foolish pining since R.J. had left. She hadn't given him a chance to forget R.J.'s name.

"Is he still chewing the rugs?" R.J. asked as he picked up the dog.

Angeline nodded. "Yeah, the vet says it's just something some breeds do."

She stepped aside to let him in. He was dressed casual, black tailored pants with a V-neck beige sweater that showed just a triangle of dark chest hair. Even with the lanky dog still in his arms, he looked like the phenomenal success that he was.

"I didn't know he had a breed," R.J. said and carried the dog in. "I thought he was just a small furry black mutt."

"He is," she replied. "But somewhere in that confusion is a breed that feasts on fabric fibers."

Angeline watched as he playfully wrestled Max to the floor. His tan skin reminded her of the bronze statues she'd studied while in Europe. His large shoulders shook with laughter as Max nipped at his face. A hint of sorrow hit her as she realized he'd missed their hound but resented having to see her again.

He straightened after several moments of playful tussling. A slight sheen of perspiration dampened his brow.

The amusement faded from his face as he looked at her. It was replaced by something foreign, something she couldn't name. But it had her quaking.

She cleared her throat. "So, I see you found the place okay?"

He nodded.

"It's pretty humid out there, isn't it?" Lord, she hated small talk.

"Yeah, I guess there's a huge storm on its way east."

"I hope the Bays' flight doesn't get canceled." She forced a smile. "Logan still shuts down at the hint of a raindrop."

He nodded, his stare intense.

She closed the door and turned to face him.

"Here." He held out his hand to her. A large stone glittered in his palm. "Your ring."

She reached for it. "I—I didn't realize you were going to get a ring. It's lovely."

"I tried to find a large one," he said. "In case Tavov and Mila are wondering why you don't always wear it, they'll just assume it's because of its large size."

"Well, it is a big stone." She picked it up, a part of her wishing he'd slip it on her finger himself.

"We have to look authentic. I rented it, along with a band for myself."

A lump formed in her throat. "I still have my original wedding ring," she admitted, unsure why.

"Oh." He cleared his throat. "Well, I needed to get one. Besides, a large diamond is far more suited to you. Always has been."

She wasn't sure how to respond to that. An uncomfortable silence settled between them. He hadn't even held on to that small symbol of their marriage. It shouldn't have disappointed her, but it did.

"Anyway," R.J. continued, "I brought over a few things so it looks like I live here when your guests arrive tomorrow." He lifted the leather carrying case in his hand. "The rest will be delivered in the morning. Just show me where I can put it and I'll have to be on my way." He was brusque, to the point. R.J. clearly didn't want to spend any more time alone with her than he had to.

"I emptied part of the closet. It's through those doors," she directed him.

She wanted him to stay. It had been so long since they had talked to each other.

"Can I get you something to drink? Some tea? Or wine? I happen to have some of the red I know you like." She happened to have it because she'd searched all of the North End's Italian district for it.

"Used to like," he corrected her. "I don't drink that anymore."

"Oh." A dull ache nestled in her chest. She didn't even know what he liked anymore.

So much for having him stay awhile.

An idea began to form. "Well. That might be

a problem," she said with more enthusiasm than she should have.

"What? That I don't drink the same wine I used to?"

"No, that we're supposed to be happily married still and we don't know anything about each other now. I think we need to discuss this. Get our stories straight for the dinner conversation tomorrow night."

She started pacing along the long coffee table in the middle of the room. Max walked with her a few steps before settling himself near the fireplace.

"There are all sorts of things I need to know about you, all kinds of questions I should ask, and vice versa."

R.J. looked uncomfortable for a moment. Letting out a deep breath, he rubbed his palm over his face. "I suppose you're right." He sat down on the sofa. "Looks like I'll need some of that wine after all," he added with a dry tone.

An almost giddy relief washed over her. He would stay. "I'll be right back," she said and ran into the kitchen.

When she returned, Max was snoring and R.J. had settled himself comfortably on the sofa.

"All right, let's start easy. How hard was it to start your firm?" she asked as she poured the glasses.

He lifted his head to look at her. "That's easy?"

"No? Okay, we'll get back to that one. What's your favorite dish now?"

"Franks and beans."

She felt her stomach turn over. "I've always hated franks and beans."

"I know."

She waved her hand. "Okay, what do you like to drink? I know it's not this anymore." She indicated the glass she was handing him.

"Ouzo. I like ouzo."

"Ouzo? Isn't that a bit hard-core?" Although it made sense, because so was he. He'd always been a firm man, but now he seemed harsher somehow, colder and more distant.

"I just got back from the Mediterranean and found I'd acquired an appreciation for it. It tastes like liquid licorice with a punch."

She tried not to turn up her nose. "I've always hated licorice."

He waited a beat. "I know."

"All right, let's move on. What music are you listening to these days?"

"A little bit of everything, really. Except Armstrong. I don't like Louis Armstrong at all. Much too lax and easy for me."

This wasn't going well. "I love Louis Armstrong."

"I know."

It dawned on her suddenly. "You're teasing me."

The corner of his mouth lifted.

She leaned a knee next to him on the couch and gave him a useless shove on the shoulder. "Robert James Davet, you've been teasing me all this time with contradictory pretend answers."

He reached up and tapped a playful finger on her nose. "I guess I must know more about you than you think."

Electricity crackled between them. She had the sudden urge to ask him the questions that were running through her mind. The same ones she'd been seeking the answers to every day for the past three years.

Is there someone special in your life now?

Has someone been lucky enough to snare your interest and attention the way I used to?

She cleared her throat. "What's the last book you've read?"

He told her, but it didn't register.

She nodded. "What do you do in your spare time?"

Do you still like to linger in bed Saturday mornings?

"Work," he answered.

That much she should have guessed. "What's been your proudest achievement?"

"The phenomenal growth of Davet Security Services."

Ditto.

"And your greatest failure?"

He hesitated, staring at her, almost looking right through her. His eyes were full of meaning. A gust of wind rattled the windows outside. Understanding dawned on her, and she felt a wrenching ache start around the area of her heart.

He was thinking about the two of them. She knew it. He was thinking their marriage was his biggest mistake.

She tried to pretend the world hadn't crashed in around her. Slowly seating herself on the ottoman in front of him, she tried to change the direction of the conversation. She would somehow get past the burning pain. "I bet you haven't changed the way you drink your coffee. Or the predawn workouts you never skipped."

He nodded.

She decided to go on. "And I'm guessing you can still ride a motorcycle like a daredevil. I bet your pool game is as smooth as it used to be. And something tells me your poker hand has lightened casino coffers all over the world these past couple of years." She looked up to see a muscle twitch in the hard set of his jaw.

He leaned toward her, a scant inches from her face. "That's right, Angel. I still have all the characteristics that made me an unfit son-in-law for the Scott dynasty."

She bit her lip. "That's not what I was getting at." Looking away, she added, "I'm so sorry for everything you were put through. My father can be a ruthless man."

R.J. sniffed an ironic laugh. "A ruthless man who had definite ideas about whom you should marry. And it wasn't anyone like me."

She should have been prepared for this, should have seen it coming. Damn her father and his ideals for her future. He'd done everything he could to make sure R.J. knew he thought he wasn't good enough. "Maybe this isn't the time to get into all this."

"Why not? Don't talk about my background?

Don't talk about who I am? Who I've always been."

"That's not what I mean." He was putting words in her mouth.

"What do you mean, then?" he asked. "You know me well enough, Angel. You know I'm South End litter, from the part of Boston people like you avoid."

"That's not true. I've always been impressed with what you've managed to accomplish despite everything. You know that."

He let out a sarcastic laugh. "Is that why you came on to me that night at the campus party? Was it some type of debutante bet? To see who could win a token from the wrong side of the city?"

She lifted her chin. "I came on to you because I wanted to. Because of the way you were looking at me."

"But we both should have known better. It was against all the rules, you were out of my league." He let out a weary sigh. "I should have stayed away from you. As your father made crystal clear."

Like it could have been so easy. "What about what we were starting to feel?"

His sharp features seemed to take on an even more angular set. She felt compelled to continue, perhaps foolishly. "I know it wasn't my imagination, R.J. I know I saw attraction in your face those first few times we ran into each other." Her voice came out in a whisper. An imaginary fist had wrapped itself around her throat, its fingers strong and relentless.

He leaned back into the cushions, putting some distance between them. "I remember you've never had a problem being bold."

She cleared her throat. "Then we have changed after all. Because I certainly don't feel that way now."

"Perhaps I'd better go."

"Are you walking out on me? Just because the conversation has gotten a little serious? Again?"

His laugh was sharp. "Now, that's an interesting question. If I recall, I asked you to come with me. As long as we're remembering, we may as well be accurate."

She sighed, trying to find a way to explain how difficult such a move would have been for her back then. "There was no easy way for me to do that. You don't understand. And you didn't then either." She noticed his fingers tighten around the glass and worried it might snap in his hand.

"So it would appear."

"Besides," she continued, "things had gotten bad for us way before you took the physical steps out the door. We had my father set against our union from the very beginning. And we were both much too focused on our professional careers. I regret that." She decided to take a chance and move forward with her next question. "Why didn't we try harder, R.J.? Why did we let outside forces drive such a wedge between us?"

He stiffened ever so slightly and set the glass down hard on the coffee table. "What does it matter now? We have to take care of this one scenario, and then the past will be dead and buried." He paused, then added, "Once again."

Angeline felt the mask of neutrality she'd put up begin to crumble, and she tried to hold on to some semblance of control. Why did his nonchalance hurt so much? It didn't take a genius to realize he wanted out as things had gotten difficult. Granted, her father's behavior toward him had been reprehensible, down to promising to cut her off entirely if they did get married. A threat her father had followed through on. Well, she'd prove to Richard Scott that she didn't need his money to be successful. He didn't have a right to meddle in her life the way he had with R.J. She couldn't let him get away with what he'd done to alienate her husband from the very beginning.

In the end, her father had won. Her marriage had crumbled. R.J. had walked away.

Angel hadn't seen or spoken to her only parent since. Unable to forgive and forget, she refused to contact her father. Not that he'd bothered to make any contact either. Apparently they were stuck in a stubborn standoff to see who would blink first. She vowed that it wouldn't be her.

In a daze, she nodded. "You're right, R.J. I agree," she lied. Her voice sounded strained even to her own ears, and she glanced at him to see if he'd noticed.

A wave of sorrow struck her for what she'd lost. Her eyes moved over his face of their own volition. Nostalgia for days gone by engulfed her, and she found herself moving closer toward him into the sofa.

His low voice reached her through a dense fog. "It was nice while it lasted. But it's ancient history now. It doesn't make sense to dwell on the past. We got married way too young. Neither one of us was ready for such a commitment."

The words barely registered. "Mmm, it was nice, though, wasn't it?" Just for a moment she allowed herself to remember the sweet, not the bitter.

Nice was a drastic understatement for the way things had been between them. They'd had everything a young couple could want. Almost.

"We were good together, weren't we?" She wanted him to say it, needed to hear him agree.

She saw something flare in his eyes and instantly recognized the familiarity of old longings.

So much time had passed, and she'd missed him. Her mind may have ignored it, but her heart had ached all the while he'd been gone. But he was here now, and he was so close. She could smell the sweet woodsy scent of the imported wine on his breath. His familiar cologne triggered long-forgotten memories in the back recesses of her brain.

Her gaze settled on his lips. Firm and full, the way she'd remembered. Would they taste the same? Would his skin hold the same texture and warmth it had years ago?

The pounding of her heart grew painful. She watched as he lifted his hands up to reach for her. What would it be like to feel his touch again? She knew the reality would blow away even the dreams she'd had every night since she'd last seen him.

The heat of his hands burned through her silk blouse as they settled around her shoulders, his touch gentle, yet strong. She moistened her lips and moved into him. All she'd have to do was reach for his mouth with hers. She inclined her head, mindless now, and ready to take what she so desperately wanted.

He started to speak, and anticipation assaulted her. He had to acknowledge the magic their marriage had once held. Despite the bitter and swift ending, despite the searing pain of loss, he had to agree that they had been happy together as man and wife once.

She wanted to taste him again, wanted his mouth on hers like they'd never been apart. She reached for him.

His lips moved. "Don't."

He said it in a strained, barely audible whisper, but the single word struck her with the force of a physical blow.

His command echoed through her desire-fogged mind, and she froze. Yanking herself out of his grasp, she turned away from the tightness in his face.

Shaking with embarrassment, she kept her back to him. Dear heavens, she'd just tried to kiss her estranged husband. And he'd literally pushed her away. "Perhaps you had better leave after all."

There was rustling behind her as he stood.

"Angel, you don't—"

She didn't let him continue. "I'll see you tomorrow, R.J. Thanks for taking time to come out tonight. By this time tomorrow, it will all be over and we can both pretend this never happened. None of it." Was she trying to reassure R.J. or herself?

She heard him let out a deep breath and moved her head sideways but couldn't bring herself to face him. He patted the sleeping dog, then made his way to the door.

"I'll see you tomorrow, then," he said.

For one final time, she thought, and a sharp hurt sliced her heart.

CHAPTER THREE

TIME ZERO. AND it was going to be a very trying night. R.J. braced himself in the hallway and tried to prepare for the upcoming evening. Stalling, he was definitely stalling.

He squeezed his eyes shut. It was one night. How hard could it be? After all, it hadn't been that long ago since he'd lived the part he was being required to play. Surely, he could act out a role he'd already experienced. So why was his head pounding?

Because he had no business even being in the same room with Angeline Scott. This was insanity, an affront to any sense of equilibrium. Hell, she'd tried to kiss him last night. How could she taunt him like that? Did she think he could be immune to her twice in one lifetime? For her own good, he swore he'd try to stay unmoved throughout this whole charade. He couldn't toy with rekindling their affections. He'd tried too hard to stay away. Angel deserved better. Because of him, her father had severed all contact with her and cut her off financially.

And any hope that the man may have changed had been shattered last year when they'd run into each other at an international business symposium. Richard Scott had made it very clear that, CEO or not, R.J. would never be in the same league as his daughter.

R.J. knew Angel had no hope of reconciling with her father unless R.J. remained out of the picture. Then maybe she'd have a chance to regain all Richard was keeping from her.

She was the sole Scott heir. How could R.J. allow himself to be the reason she lost that? In fact, if it wasn't for him, Angel would have access to all the financial resources she needed right now to ensure her company survived. But she'd lost it all. For him.

He had to make that right.

He also had to purge all of that from his thoughts at the moment. It only served to agitate him further, and he couldn't afford that right now. Tonight, it was all for show.

He used the key she'd given him to enter the apartment. The aroma of home cooking and a bristling fire hit him as he stepped in. Sudden, almost painful nostalgia overwhelmed his senses. He had entered their studio apartment countless times like this. Back then the various scents from the kitchen had been more mundane. Usually plain pasta or some meat roasting in the oven. Angel's culinary skills weren't quite enviable at that point, but she'd tried and he'd loved the attempts. He'd loved her for trying.

Without warning, she breezed into the living room through the swing door of the kitchen. As she spotted him, the silver tray in her hand slightly tilted off balance.

"You're here," she stated.

"Just walked in."

She set her load down on the cocktail table. "The Bays are set to arrive in a few minutes."

He took in the snug fit of her feminine tuxedo-cut black suit. The form-fitting jacket accented her waist. The lace camisole she had underneath peaked at the V below her neck and practically screamed *temptation*. His hand tightened around the wine bottle he was holding.

"You can set that in the kitchen," she ordered, and then moved with catlike grace to the mantel and lifted the silver candle set.

Without responding, R.J. made his way into the

kitchen. This night was not going to be over soon enough. She'd always been stunning, but he realized that now she was in her element. He set the wine bottle down and braced his palms on the counter in front of him. Dark, thick clouds moved through the window above the sink.

The storm was moving closer. He would have to make sure to still the one brewing inside him.

This was why he couldn't be around her. This burning need to touch her, to claim her as his. It was the same insanity that had nearly destroyed both of them in the past, when they'd let physical desire rule their better judgment. By the time he found out how mismatched they were, the damage had been done. The memory of that pain should have been enough to guarantee he'd keep his distance tonight.

He walked back out into the living room just as the doorbell rang. Angel froze in the act of lighting a candle. The fiery glow of the forgotten match threw shadows over her face. Her eyes sparkled before the flame.

He took her palm and blew the match out. "We better let them in, don't you think?"

"I—I guess so."

"You guess so? It's kind of late to back out now,

Angel." He was still trying to ascertain just how far they had come and how he would manage to recover.

"Why would I want to back out? I just need to tell them this little white lie until I can prove to them what good hands their tea plants are in. By then they won't care anymore."

"And if they do care?"

She gave a quick shake of her head. "I can't worry about that now. I'll need to think about it later." She threw a slight Southern accent in imitation of the famous *Gone with the Wind* line.

He smiled. "In that case, Scarlett, I'll go let the Yankees in."

She nodded and swallowed. It was surprising to see her so nervous. She'd been the most self-assured woman he'd ever known. Granted, the circumstances were a little unusual, but something was throwing Angel off like he'd never witnessed before.

He had to wonder- could it have anything to do with him?

Of course not. She was worried about her business. She was worried about failing to continue the jobs program for all the women who worked for her.

He took a deep breath as he went to answer the door then yanked it open. A smiling, middle-aged couple stared up at him. Both of them had dark hair, hers a shade less brown. They both smiled wide, warmth exuding their features.

"Good evening," R.J. said as he stepped aside to let them in. "I'm Angeline's husband." He nearly choked on the last word.

Angel strode toward them, beaming a warm, welcoming smile. She seemed to have recovered from her earlier nervousness. "Tavov. Mila. So nice to see you again. Please come in."

R.J. felt her hand on his arm and flinched. He tried not to look affected. There was nothing unusual about a wife taking her husband by the arm as they greeted guests.

Man, it was going to be the longest night of his life.

"Nice to see you, too, dear. And very nice to finally meet you." The older man flashed a wide, friendly grin as he turned to R.J. He stretched out his free hand, giving R.J. a welcome excuse to free his own arm. "We weren't sure we'd ever catch up to you," he continued.

"Tavov, Mila. Very nice to meet you both," R.J.

spoke over Angel's head as Mrs. Bay had her in an affectionate hug. "I'm R.J."

"Did you have any trouble getting here?" Angel inquired, still locked in the embrace.

"None at all. The driver was waiting for us right at the gate where we landed," Tavov replied.

Before R.J. knew what was happening, Mila moved toward him and he found himself in the same bear hug he'd just witnessed. A stab of guilt hit him at the way he was deceiving such warm, genuine people.

One look at Angel's pale face told him she was thinking the same thing. For one insane moment he wished with all his heart that it could have been different. That the charade had not been necessary.

Where had that thought come from? He didn't have time to speculate. An awkward silence had settled around the foursome. Angel appeared to be frozen in her spot. So far, they weren't doing a very good job of personifying the perfect American couple.

"Why don't we move inside?" He guided the older couple in front of him. Waiting a beat for Angel to catch up, he cupped her elbow and pulled her to his side.

She was shaking. A sheen of perspiration had formed above her lip. He remembered that to be a bad sign. At this rate she wasn't going to be able to go through with it. He gave her hand what he hoped was a reassuring squeeze. She leaned into him, and without thinking, he moved his arm around her waist.

He just held her, close to him, as if his closeness could absorb her anxiety somehow. In a moment, her breathing seemed to even, and he started to lead her toward the living room, where the other couple had seated themselves.

"It's all right," he whispered in her ear. "It will all be over soon."

"I know, it's just—I'd almost forgotten what nice people they were." She wrung her hands. "I wish it hadn't come to this."

He dropped his arm. A sudden sense of loss hit him as soon as he did so. She felt so right near him, up against him. She always had.

"You'll tell them the truth soon enough. For now, let's go take care of business, all right?" He gave her a small nudge forward and followed her in.

Angel composed herself enough to start serving the hors d'oeuvres.

"Tavov, Mila," she began. "It's so lovely to have you here finally. How was your trip?" she asked over her shoulder as she held the tray out to R.J. He shook his head to decline. Somehow he couldn't quite summon up an appetite.

"Oh, it was pretty uneventful," Mila answered. "But it's always so exciting when we come to the States. So much changes, yet it's always the same. The energy level you Americans have, it's just harrowing."

"We should all slow down a little bit. It can get a little tiring to be on the go all the time."

"Yes, my goodness, dear. I can imagine it can be exhausting," Mila agreed.

"What we could use is that soothing herbal tea in this part of the world," Angel said as she set the tray down and sat. He had to hand it to her. She knew how to segue.

"I can't argue with you there, young lady," Tavov stated. "That's why we're here."

"Well, I'm anxious to start talking about it myself. How is the latest crop of Mila's Bloom faring?"

"She hasn't stopped talking about it since she got back," R.J. added. He was pretty certain it was true enough.

She looked up and sent him a smile. A jolt of pleasure shot through clear to his toes. How adolescent of him, he thought.

"Well, it is turning into a pretty impressive crop." Tavov nodded.

Angel jumped up in her seat. "Excellent. So we'll be ready to start shipping when I come down for the harvest?"

Mila squinted her eyes and smiled. "That's what I love about you, Angeline. Always assuming the sale."

Angel had the decency to look sheepish. Then she lifted her head and gave R.J. a pointed look full of meaning. "I've managed to acquire some invaluable things that way."

For an instant, silence took over the small room as the two of them just stared at each other. R.J. couldn't seem to pull his eyes away. When he finally did, he watched as Mila's smile turned into a wide grin.

"How romantic." Mila laughed. "And to think, you gave us the impression originally that you were a staunch businesswoman with no mind for family or roots. And it's so confusing that your last names aren't the same."

"That's not uncommon in the States, Mila," R.J.

responded. "A lot of women prefer to keep their birth names for professional reasons."

Tavov swallowed the last bit of his shrimp cocktail. "Well, we make it a point to deal only with family-run operations. We've found things are much more stable that way. Remember the last fiasco with that European businessman?" he asked his wife as he patted her knee.

Mila nodded. "Oh, it was awful. That man was much more concerned with turning a fast profit than nurturing a business. All the more resources to buy his bachelor toys. We swore we wouldn't make that mistake again."

"That's why we're so glad to see how happy the two of you are together," Tavov said. R.J. noticed Angel's slight cringe.

"You know, dear, they remind me of another young couple," Mila spoke to her husband.

"They do." Tavov beamed as he turned back to her and R.J. "We happen to have a major event to look forward to. Our groundskeeper's son is marrying our cropper's daughter. Two of the sweetest kids. So in love. We're holding the ceremony right on our estate."

"That's quite generous of you," Angel said.

"Nonsense," Tavov retorted. "We're almost

more excited than they are about it. The ceremony will fall right on the week that you're visiting us, Angel. I'm sure they'd love it if you could join us. Practically the whole town will be there."

Angel's expression became wistful, but it disappeared an instant later. "I would be honored. And I wish them every happiness together," she said.

Mila nodded. "They seem very happy to have found each other. Those two are very committed, as if they just know they were meant for each other."

Then they'd be rare exceptions, R.J. thought. A sudden flash of lightning tore through the sky in the window behind the Bays. The storm was going to be a furious one.

Mila leaned closer to him. "So tell me, R.J., what's your secret?"

"Uh, secret?"

She smiled. "Yes, how did you know that Angeline was the one for you?"

Angel prayed for a strong gust of wind to tear the roof off and suck her right out of the apartment. This was excruciating. Mila Bay was actually asking R.J. about their relationship. R.J., the same man who hadn't even held on to his wedding band.

She stood up quickly, sparing him the discomfort of having to answer.

"What's wrong with me? You two must be starving after such a long journey. Let's get started with dinner. R.J., would you show our guests to the table?"

He moved toward the dining table and pulled out Mila's chair. Then he motioned for Tavov to sit down. Just as if he was the true man of the house.

"Excuse me while I start to serve."

R.J. cleared his throat behind her. "I'll help you."

They both moved into the kitchen. Angeline couldn't get to the sink fast enough. Splashing water on her face, she turned to catch R.J. watching her, his arms crossed in front of his chest.

"What?"

"Why are you getting so nervous? It's going great."

"Great? You think this is going great? Our guest just asked you to tell her what makes us such a great couple."

He grinned. "I could have come up with something."

She walked over to him, entranced by the way

his smile transformed his face. "Oh? And what would you have said?"

"I would have said that you fell madly in love with me on sight and I couldn't get rid of you for anything."

Angel opened her mouth wide in shock, then saw his mischievous grin. She poked his chest with her index finger. "You wouldn't have dared."

He grabbed her wrist playfully and pulled her toward him. "Wouldn't I?"

"R.J., if you had said something ridiculous like that, I'd, I'd—"

He pulled her closer, an amused glint dancing in his eyes. "You'd what?"

"I'd have laughed in your face."

He gave an exaggerated shudder. "Ooh, violent."

His sarcasm was not lost on her. "Then, I would have pretended to accidentally spill hot soup into your lap."

The grin faded. "You wouldn't."

She shrugged. "You sure about that?"

"That would hurt."

"That's the point."

He seemed to contemplate that for a moment, then let go of her hand. "All right, I'll try not to make any snide comments."

She laughed when he gave her a painfully put-upon look. "Why, thank you."

He returned the smile, and it was so easy to remember all the reasons she'd fallen so hard for him. Nothing she'd experienced before or since had even come close to what they'd shared.

"Just be careful with that soup." R.J.'s mock reprimand pulled her back into the present. "Actually," he said as he moved toward the stove, "I think I'll serve it."

Angel watched him walk back out to the dining area carrying the serving dish. Still giggling, she was only vaguely aware that their little exchange had lessened her anxiety.

Minutes later they were all seated around the table, the aroma of cream of asparagus wafting up from the plates.

"Angel mentioned that you own a corporate security firm," Mila directed to R.J., then blew on her spoonful of hot soup.

"Yes, that's my primary focus right now. Angel heads most of the operations for TeaLC."

He had managed to answer the question without one lie.

"Such a dynamic field, network security," Tavov

said. "I imagine something as trivial as tea distribution isn't very exciting to you."

Uh-oh. Angel swallowed. "More soup for anyone? R.J., I see you're done already." She started to stand.

"No, Angel. I'll hold off until the main course." He braced his elbows on the table and leaned toward the other man. "On the contrary, Tavov. I find my wife's side of the business fascinating. But I would never presume to understand as much about it as she does. She's the brains behind TeaLC. She always has been. I can only be impressed by her tremendous success."

Angel blinked at R.J.'s answer. He was impressed with her as a businesswoman? She gave a mental shake of her head and spread her napkin back on her lap.

R.J. was playing his part as the doting husband. And he was doing it quite well. It was no more than that. He might sound convincing, but she couldn't forget how fictional all this was.

Tavov seemed mollified.

Angel let out the breath she was holding and pushed back her chair. "Excuse me, I'm just going to go get the entrée. We're having grilled salmon with a parsley glaze. And pasta. I hope that's okay with everyone."

"That sounds delicious, dear," Mila answered.

"Just be careful serving the glaze." R.J. winked.

She gave him what she hoped was an admonishing glare, then turned toward the kitchen. The smile she was trying to keep from forming on her face broke free as soon as she turned her back.

Forty-five minutes later, Angel rolled the serving tray with all the dishes into the kitchen. They could be rinsed in the morning.

Rejoining her guests in the living room, she walked over to the stereo. "I think we could use some music." She pressed the selection on her entertainment center. Moments later the mellowing notes of classic Armstrong filled the room.

"Why, that's a lovely tune you have playing, Angeline," Mila commented.

"I'm glad you like it. It's one of my favorites."

"Just beautiful." Mila smiled at Angeline. "I remember you telling us how much you and R.J. enjoy dancing together. Tavov and I don't do much of it anymore."

"Was that a shameless way to get me to ask you to dance, my dear?" Tavov asked with humor, then stood up. He extended his hand to his wife. "Well, I'll do it only if Angeline and R.J. join us."

Angel tried not to wince. R.J. was probably cursing the forces that had ever brought them together. Here he was being urged into dancing with an estranged wife he thought he'd been rid of years ago.

"I—I'm not in a dancing mood tonight," Angel hedged, trying to make things easy for him.

"Please," Mila insisted. "You don't know what it takes to get this man to dance."

"I really don't think it's—"

R.J. stood before she could finish. In disbelief, she watched him extend his hand to her.

"What do you say, Princess? Shall we dance?"

She looked up at him, at a loss for words. The first time he'd ever touched her, he had uttered those very same words. The double meaning in his invitation had been clear, then.

Lost in memories, she stepped into his embrace. The older couple started to dance next to them.

It felt so right. He felt so good. The way it had every time he'd touched her. Their bodies molded perfectly, their rhythms completely in tune. Apparently they still moved well together.

Her feelings must have shown on her face, because he pulled her closer. Her chest molded tightly on his.

She instinctively rested her cheek on his chest, his heartbeat rhythmically pounding up against her ear. She'd always loved dancing with him, swaying in his arms. Every weekend while in school, they would move together to the sounds of cool, slow jazz at one of the clubs around campus. She longed for those days when she'd really been his partner, on the dance floor and everywhere else.

Their first dance had been nothing less than thrilling for her. After weeks of her trying futilely to get his attention, he'd finally talked to her. She'd kidded him about it that night.

Oh, you had my attention, all right. Let's just say I have this silly quirk about self-preservation.

She shut her eyes against the memories. How could she have lost a man like this? How could she have been lucky enough to find him and foolish enough not to hold on to him? She sighed into his chest and felt his arms tighten around her.

"We'd better be careful," he whispered into her ear, his breath thick and hot against her skin. "We get in trouble when we dance together."

"If I recall," she started in a low voice, "it wasn't the dancing that got us into trouble."

He laughed softly. "Maybe not, but it didn't help. Logic seemed to fly out the window whenever I had you in my arms."

"Like now?"

He pulled his head back to look at her. She wet her lips when his gaze fell to them. She saw his expression harden, the arms around her suddenly becoming much more lax.

"We're different people now."

They certainly were. Now, rather than seeing desire in R.J.'s face, all she could see was self-condemnation. For what? For having to touch her? For allowing himself into such a position that he'd had to dance with her three years after separating?

"People can't change so much so quickly, can they?"

"Maybe not. Maybe they just face tests that bring out their true priorities."

There was no bitterness in the statement. Just what sounded like pure acceptance. It made her realize how much distance there truly was between them. As far as R.J. was concerned, they had made their decisions years ago. Even though he really hadn't given her much of a choice.

The song came to an end. R.J.'s hands drifted slowly down her arms and rested gently on her waist. She moved her hands lower on his shoulders, and for a moment they both just stood still. Finally, R.J. stepped back, and she could have sworn her feet hadn't touched the floor until then.

"Well, little lady," Tavov said to his wife, "we've had a long day. What do you say we make our way to our hotel and retire?"

Mila sighed. "Yes, I suppose it's getting late."

"That it is, dear."

Angeline forced herself to step away from R.J. and turned to her guests. "Then I guess I'll see the two of you at our lunch meeting tomorrow."

The digital audio player behind them switched to the next track, "Fantastic, That's You." Angeline guided the other couple toward the door. She could only hope that they didn't notice the moisture gleaming in her eyes.

CHAPTER FOUR

IT WAS OVER.

Angeline moved to join R.J. where he stood in front of the window watching the fall of the rain.

"I guess that went as well as we could have hoped," she said, doing her best to sound casual.

R.J. merely nodded.

The jazzy melody sounding from the stereo momentarily succumbed to the thunder outside. The evening had gone off without any glitches. But Angeline didn't feel much like celebrating.

"Looks like a nasty storm."

As if on cue, the lights flickered, then resumed their full brightness.

"Did you park far?" she asked.

"Yeah. I did." He moved to the bar and set his glass down. "I better start making my way back, come to think of it."

She could only wait silently as he grabbed his bag from the closet.

He wasn't looking at her when he came back

into the room. "I think that's everything," he said. "I guess I'll see you around."

Before the words were out of his mouth, another round of lightning pulsated through the dimly lit room. The lights gave one more flicker, then went out completely. Heavy rain pelted the glass windows.

"It looks like you may be too late."

She heard a sigh of pure weariness. He didn't say anything.

"You don't want to be walking out in that mess," she spoke into the dark.

"I don't have a choice. It doesn't look like it's going to let up anytime soon."

Angeline knew he was close enough to touch. "You could wait it out."

He was quiet for a moment. She couldn't decide whether she was fortunate or not in not being able to see him. "Here? I don't think so," he finally answered.

"R.J., there really is no reason why you shouldn't. We're both adults. It's silly to risk storm and cold when there's plenty of room here. I might even be able to dig out one of your old pajamas."

"You held on to my pajamas?"

A nervous laugh escaped her before she could stop it. "You know what a pack rat I can be."

"No, that's okay. I have to leave, Angel. I should go right now." But she knew he hadn't moved. "Listen, it was great seeing you again. I hope this all works out for you."

"Wait! We're not finished yet. I mean, I still have my part of the bargain."

"The bargain?"

"I'm going to help you expand into Europe. Remember? Our deal."

He cleared his throat. "We can talk about that later. I'll have my assistant call you or something."

She felt her legs start to weaken. He was going to walk out of her life again. And there wasn't a thing she could do about it. He didn't want to deal with her directly about the expansion. Hell, he wanted nothing more to do with her.

While she still felt the burn on her skin from his touch.

"At least let me walk you down. Just let me find a flashlight."

Just give me a few more moments.

Distracted by his closeness and stumbling in the dark, she turned to make her way into the kitchen.

A loud thump followed by a sharp pain told her she'd walked right into her coffee table.

"Ow!"

"What is it?"

"My shin."

"Your shin?"

"Yeah, it's what I use to find things in the dark."

She heard his small laugh. "Are you all right?"

"Yes," she lied. "This is just all so awkward."

"Yeah, I know. Who would have thought that we'd ever be in such a strange predicament when we saw each other again?"

She remembered a time when awkwardness hadn't existed between them. They'd watched numerous storms together, holding each other.

"Funny how things turned out in the end," he added.

The end. "Yes, well, let me go find that flashlight."

An agonizingly short time later, they were out in the front lobby of her building. A few emergency lamps and the streetlights outside afforded the only light.

"Well, goodbye, Angel," R.J. said suddenly. The next moment, she was watching him exit out the revolving door.

Her heart took over before she could rationalize. She wrapped her suit jacket tighter around her and ran out after him. Thick pelts of cold rain shocked her the instant she stepped outside.

"R.J., wait."

He stopped and slowly turned around. She moved closer, the cold starting to make her shiver. Now that she'd stopped him she didn't know what she wanted to say.

He spoke first. "Angel, get back inside. You're getting soaked."

"It's okay," she insisted, though her chattering teeth said otherwise. "It just occurred to me that I never really thanked you, I mean tonight."

His eyes searched her face. What in the world must he be thinking? What exactly did she want him to say? You're welcome?

"Really," she went on, feeling completely foolish. "You went above and beyond the norm."

Then she did the only thing she could think of—she extended her hand and waited for him to shake it.

Somehow she'd ended up shivering in a cold, powerful storm, shaking hands with R. J. Davet. And chances were very good she'd never see him again.

* * *

He was gone. Angeline stepped inside her dark apartment and closed the door behind her. Her ceiling lights flickered, then came back on, once again illuminating the normally cheery decor. Except now the place looked empty, in a way it never had before.

She should be elated that they were finally done with this insanity, that the Bays hadn't suspected the truth. Instead she wanted to huddle in a dark corner. Forever. She couldn't help but feel low for deceiving such warm people. Yes, technically she wasn't lying, but she certainly wasn't exactly telling them the whole truth.

But none of this was really for her own benefit. She was doing it for all her employees. For all those deserving women who had no one else and nowhere else to turn to. When would she ever get another opportunity like this to secure her employees' futures in such a long-term way?

The reminder did little to lessen her misery. She felt downright unsettled. As if she'd forgotten something crucial after leaving for a trip but couldn't remember what it might be. If only R.J. had stayed longer. It would be so helpful to be able to talk to him right now. To explain why she'd had to go through with tonight.

She could call him. Just to talk. Explain her motivation, make things clearer.

She had her phone in her hands before she stopped herself. With disgust, she threw it against the back cushion of her couch. What in the world was she doing? Her pride was all she had left. For heaven's sake. She'd already run after the man in the middle of a lightning storm.

She had to accept that it was over. Her business was all that mattered now, and it allowed her to help those less fortunate. There was absolutely no reason to doubt her life. It was exactly the way she wanted it. She'd worked very hard to get here and had no reason to feel guilty. Sometimes the end did justify the means.

She forced herself to step away from the door and walked back toward her bedroom. Max lay snoring at the foot of her bed, and Angeline quietly tiptoed around him. At least R.J. had not fought for custody. How much loss could one girl take?

She undressed quickly, too tired to do anything but throw her wet clothes on the floor. Pulling her thick flannel nightgown over her head, she crawled into bed.

She wasn't going to cry. Damn it, she wouldn't. No matter what it took. Her marriage was over. She'd been through crying over it years ago. And she was going to stop tossing and turning this minute and get some sleep.

A knock on the door stopped her midtoss.

R.J. It had to be. She sucked in a gasp of air. He wasn't going to leave after all! Possibilities started running through her head as she flung the covers away. She'd known it all along. He didn't want to leave things this unsettled between them either.

Struggling to maintain both a steady breath and her composure, she ran back into the other room. Every sense she possessed told her it was him knocking.

She pulled the door open. "R.J., it's you."

His eyes traveled over her, and he lifted an eyebrow. "I see you've changed your sleeping attire over the years."

"You decided to come back."

He ran a hand through the soaking-wet hair now curling with dampness. "I had to, Angel. I couldn't leave."

"You couldn't?" Her breath caught, her chest

hurt. He hadn't been able to walk away after all. He was back to see things through this time.

"Yeah, the damn roads are starting to flood already," he said as he stepped inside. "They've blocked all traffic onto Storrow." He shrugged out of his suit jacket and threw it onto the sofa with clear frustration.

He was here only because the roads were blocked.

"I see." This time she really did see. She saw clearly her foolishness in pining for something she'd already lost. His reason for coming back had nothing to do with her.

His next words only drove it home. "Listen, the whole street is dark. I'm not going to try to drive through the city tonight. I'll call around to see which hotels have power. Where are the Bays staying? I'll be sure to steer clear of that one."

She steeled herself as all last traces of hope fled. "Now you're being silly. A hotel is hardly necessary." Turning, she spoke with her back to him. "I have a guest room you're welcome to use. You can leave in the morning."

"Don't go out of your way, Angel. This isn't a sleepover. As soon as the roads clear, I'll be on my way."

She walked over to the hall closet and grabbed a large terry towel. "I expected nothing more, R.J. And believe me. I'm not going out of my way." Not anymore, she thought and flung the towel toward him. He caught it with one hand.

"The guest room's down the hall," she continued. "There's a bathroom off of it. My bedroom is across the hall if you need anything. Have a good night. And if I don't see you in the morning, thanks once again for your help."

By the time her head hit her pillow, the trail of tears on her face was completely dry. Closing her eyes, she waited for the painful, poignant memories to revisit her like spirits in the night.

Dreams born of memories were the most restless kind.

What in the world was that incessant pounding?

Angeline pulled the covers over herself and prayed for the noise to go away. She couldn't have been asleep more than a few minutes. And now someone was trying to torture her with loud knocking.

The door. Someone was at the door, and apparently whoever it was had no plans to go away.

Grabbing her silk robe around her, she ran to answer it. The hum of the running guest shower told her R.J. hadn't left yet. A month ago she would have sooner dropped dead than bet that Robert James Davet would be showering again in her apartment. A twinge of sadness hit her at the less than intimate reason for his stay.

"Hang on. Hang on." The scolding she intended for the offensive knocker died on her lips as she yanked the door open. The woman on the other side was not someone she expected to see.

"May I come in?"

Angeline quickly recovered and stepped aside. "Mila. By all means."

"I'm sorry," Mila began as she walked past her. "I know it's early. I wanted to get here before Tavov awoke."

"Is everything all right?" Angeline asked and shut the door. Was Mila suspicious? If so, did she have it in her to bluff?

"Actually that's what I wanted to ask you, dear." She sat down on the sofa.

Angeline knew she should offer her tea or something, but curiosity overrode her manners. "I beg your pardon? I'm not sure what you mean."

"Well, for starters, do you need to talk to someone?" Genuine compassion shone in her eyes.

"I'm sorry, I don't understand." Her mouth had gone dry. Mila appeared truly concerned about her, though she had no idea why. Angeline felt even guiltier than she had last night.

Mila cleared her throat. "Let me explain. My husband and I were having so much fun here last night. We didn't want the evening to end. So we stopped for a drink and to watch the storm before heading to our hotel." She paused before adding, "At the tavern across the street."

Across the street.

Mila continued. "Right before all the lights went out, we noticed your husband leaving. He was carrying what appeared to be a small suitcase."

"I see." Angel sat down on automatic pilot.

"Then we saw you chase after him, and—this is the part that confuses me—the two of you shook hands. Even in the dark it was easy to tell you were upset. So I wanted to come see if you were all right."

"I—uh—don't know what to say." At least that was the absolute truth.

"Now this morning," Mila continued. "I can't help but notice that you've been crying. Tavov will just say I'm a nosy old woman, but I couldn't help but be concerned. We feel we've gotten to know you a little bit, and the two of you just looked so happy last night." She leaned forward. "Is everything all right between you and R.J.?"

Don't panic. Stay cool. Angel took a deep breath to try to calm herself. It was almost humorous. Everything had almost gone off so perfectly. How coincidental that something as happenstance as a storm would wreck the whole effort. This was it, she had to confess everything. And fond of her or not, Mila and Tavov would never go through with the business deal after she told them.

She cleared her throat and prepared herself for what was to follow.

R.J. picked that moment to walk into the room. Only a towel covered him, hung low around his hips. Even in the state she was in, she couldn't help but notice the complete magnificence he exuded. Droplets of silver water glimmered on his chest. His dark hair was dripping.

"Mila." The one word sounded more like a question than a greeting. "What are you doing here so early? Everything okay?" If R.J. had noted Mila's shocked expression, he wasn't showing it.

"R.J., you're here," she said, confusion still etched in her voice.

R.J. shrugged. "Of course I'm here," he said, then blandly added, "Why are you here?"

Angel cleared her throat. "Mila and Tavov saw you leave last night," she explained. She tried to implore him across the room for forgiveness. He was going to hate her for what was about to happen.

"I do have a confession to make," she began.

R.J. snapped his head up. He lifted his eyebrows as if to ask her if she was certain. Angel took a deep breath, ready to proceed. This charade had gone far enough.

"Are you sure you want to admit it, Angel? Surely they won't be able to tell the difference. After all, they had no idea last night."

Angeline nearly moaned aloud. Dear God, he didn't have to blurt it out without giving her a chance to explain. She opened her mouth to spill out the awful truth. R.J.'s voice stopped her.

"All right, then," he continued. "I suppose we had better tell you." He moved toward the center of the room, crossing his arms in front of his wide, bare chest. "The fact of the matter is, the meal last night was catered."

Mila squinted her eyes. "That's it? That's the confession?"

R.J. walked behind Angeline and settled his hands tenderly on her shoulders. "It's part of it. The truth is, normally we would have prepared a meal together, but it's been hard to find time for such things lately. As a result—" he gave her shoulders a gentle squeeze and sighed "—our relationship has been a little strained."

Shock at the strange turn of the conversation along with the intimacy of his gesture prevented any words from forming on Angeline's lips.

"We had a bit of a spat last night," he continued. "I'm embarrassed to admit I stormed out afterward, somewhat childishly."

That was rich. Angeline couldn't imagine him ever acting in a childish way. Not even when he was an actual child. But Mila appeared to be buying it.

"That's what you witnessed last night. But I regretted it almost instantly and came back. We vowed to work on our marriage." His tone still held just the right amount of politeness to maintain a cord of amicability, but there was no mistaking the determination underneath. No one would question such a tone of voice.

How did the man manage to exude such authority wearing nothing but a large bath towel? Even standing there half-naked, there was no mistaking the man who had gone from the barest of beginnings to owning his own corporation.

"I said some things I shouldn't have said," he went on. "But I've promised to make it up to her. As soon as we decide where to go, I'm taking her away for a nice vacation. So we can get away together."

Oh, dear. Now he was outright lying for her.

Mila put a hand to her chest. "Oh, I'm so glad to hear it. Aside from our desire to form a partnership with a family operation, we've grown quite fond of Angeline over the past few months. I know I sound foolish, but I had to come make sure you were okay, Angeline." She stood up and grabbed her bag. "I'll just leave you two to go about your morning, then."

Angeline's shoulders nearly sagged with relief. Finally, she found her tongue. "No, it doesn't sound foolish at all. I really appreciate how concerned you were for me, Mila."

The older woman smiled affectionately. "Well, you've come to mean more to us than a mere business associate, you know." R.J. dropped his hands from her, and the two women started walking to the door.

"Besides," she continued, "we couldn't have had you depressed on your visit to sign the papers." She suddenly stopped midstride and turned around.

"Wait, I have a terrific idea." She glanced first to R.J. then to Angeline. "Why doesn't R.J. join you when you come?"

Oh, no. Angeline swallowed the lump of apprehension that shot through her at Mila's words. She had to stop this drastic turn at the curve. "Well, um, he has a very demanding schedule. I don't know how we'd ever be able to swing it."

Mila's expression turned crestfallen. "But I thought you said you were planning a trip and that you just had to decide where. Perhaps I'm biased, but there isn't a more peaceful or relaxing spot on earth as far as I'm concerned."

"Yes, but who knows when he'll actually be able to clear the time."

Mila gave a dismissive shake of her hand. "Nonsense, we're very flexible. There're weeks still before the harvest. You can postpone your trip and come down when it's convenient for both of you."

"We just can't," Angeline insisted, unable to come up with any more excuses.

Mila looked utterly confused. "Well, why not?"

She turned to R.J. for an answer, apparently giving up on Angeline.

Dear God, what must he be thinking now? She wouldn't be surprised if the firm hands resting gently on her neck a moment ago were itching to strangle it.

She laid a hand on Mila's arm, praying she would understand. "Fine, I need to level with you—"

R.J.'s baritone cut through her admission. It was about time he said something and aided her in averting this disaster. "I'll have my secretary clear my schedule next week. That way, Angel, you won't have to bother postponing."

She whirled around. "What?"

"I said, I'd love to accompany you. We can't turn down such a lovely gesture, now, can we?" His eyes seemed to dare her to deny it.

"What about your business? What about your expansion into Europe?"

What about the fact that we're not really even together?

"I'm ahead of plan on almost everything. This actually would be a perfect time to focus some attention to your side of the holdings."

"That's more like it. I think you're making a very wise decision," Mila said behind her.

Wise was the last word for what R.J. had just done. There would be no way out of this one. One look at Mila's expression made it clear—any attempt to back out of this commitment would be fatal for the pretense.

It was impossible to tear her eyes off R.J.'s face. She couldn't quite interpret the look he was giving her. If she didn't know better, she could have sworn it was one of reassurance.

"Mila's right, Angel. Besides, it's about time I became more than a silent partner." He looked back to the other woman. "Please include my office in the travel arrangements. My wife will give you the requisite information and a name to contact. Now, if you'll excuse me, I have some appointments this morning."

Not sparing either of them another glance, he walked back toward the hall, leaving Mila smiling.

And leaving Angeline gaping in shocked confusion.

R.J. squeezed out a dollop of shaving cream and stared at his face in the mirror. He had to focus solely on the task at hand. In due time he would think about what he had just committed himself to. But not right now.

Oh, he'd wanted to help her. He'd pretty much decided that the day in her office when she'd first asked him. Even before Shanna had cornered him, he knew he would be returning to present Angel with other options.

After all, he was one of the reasons she was in this mess. But it never occurred to him he'd actually take the masquerade to such new heights himself.

But he owed her this. Angeline would have access to all the wealth and resources of the Scott dynasty if she hadn't been cut off by her father.

He shook his head. What a mess.

Furthermore, these days that area of the world wasn't exactly the safest. With all the global turmoil, he'd be worried sick about her going alone. She might not be his wife anymore, but he still felt an obligation to make sure she was safe. They'd shared a lot during their brief union as man and wife.

See, all very sound and logical reasons.

He forced his mind back to his shaving and applied the razor to his face. Up, down. Up, down.

He heard Angel's footsteps approaching. Damn, he should have shut the door. He didn't have any explanations for her yet. Hell, he couldn't fully explain to himself what he'd just done. How would he begin to tell her that he felt as if he owed her something? Felt as if he had to make it up to her for choosing him? At first anyway.

And Richard Scott wasn't one to forgive and forget. That had been made very clear when they'd run into each other. CEO or not, R. J. Davet would never be a fit son-in-law for the Scott dynasty. He'd never fit in at the yacht club or the exclusive charity auctions. Even if he could now afford it. Nor should he have ever had the gall to think he could.

Richard Scott was certain R.J. would never be worth anything when it came to what counted: breeding and class.

Pretty much echoing everything his own old man had been saying to him his entire life. Only in more educated terms. Plus, his father had liked to make his point with physical blows for emphasis.

Angel knocked with hesitation before entering. "We need to talk, R.J."

He offered her a glance before returning his concentration to his remaining stubble. "You think?"

She brought long fingers to her mouth. Angeline Scott at a loss for words, twice already. Another subtle difference since she'd been his wife. How many other changes had he missed?

"I never meant for your involvement to get so complicated."

"We didn't appear to have much choice, though, did we?"

She started chewing her lip. "We do have a choice. I'll tell her the truth. I can't expect you to drop everything you're doing and travel to the ends of the earth with me."

"And what happens to your deal if we don't?"

"I'm guessing it will be dead in the water."

He shrugged. "All right, then, it looks like we'll be taking a trip."

She touched his shoulder, and he tried to ignore the resulting electricity. "But you don't have to do this. I'll figure out another way."

He shrugged. "It was my doing. I should have never mentioned taking a trip together. That comment gave her the idea in the first place."

"None of this is your fault," she argued. But she was oh so wrong about that.

"Well, we started this sham, we have to finish it. Besides, you said so yourself, Angel. There is no other way to get your expansion."

"I know that," she said. "But I realize now what a mistake all this was. There's no need to push it any further."

"Yeah? How are you going to explain it all to the Bays?" He waited, knowing she had no answer. "The only option is to go through with this trip and act like the committed, devoted couple."

"We both know it's not that simple. We would need Academy Award–level talent to pull something like that off. I don't know about you, but I'm not that comfortable with my thespian skills."

"You'll have to brush up on those skills quickly."

"This whole thing was a foolish, thoughtless endeavor." She pulled her hair back off her forehead, agitated. "I don't know what I was thinking. I just, I mean, all I thought about was the people who depended on TeaLC for their living. All I could see as the deal was falling through were the faces of those women when they first come in for placement. And the transformation that happens afterward, once they realize someone is willing to invest in them."

She maneuvered herself closer to the bathtub

behind him and sat down on its edge. "R.J., some of these women have no work experience. They can't even get a low-paying waitressing job. And in no time, with the dedication and hard work they usually display, they're managing whole centers, or working out of corporate. All they needed was that push."

He turned to face her. "I know, Angel. And I should tell you I'm really impressed that you went out on a limb for what you felt was important."

She blinked. "Do you really mean that?"

"I know the work and effort it takes to keep a business running. Setting up a whole work placement program on top of all that showed real dedication."

"And that surprised you?"

He shook his head slowly. "Not really. I know you're the kind of person who makes even business decisions with her heart." That knowledge only added to the guilt he felt now. How much would she be capable of if she still had the backing of her father?

She seemed surprised by his words. Silence descended on the small bathroom as his eyes locked on hers.

He wanted to touch her, burned to. She was

completely disheveled. The white robe around her looked about three sizes too big. Her hair was a mess of curls, her lips red from the way she'd been chewing them. He wanted to soothe those lips with his own. He wanted to taste her skin as he trailed kisses down her neck.

She took a small breath and he reflexively moved toward her.

A small clanging noise behind him startled him back to his senses. The razor had fallen to the floor.

Steady there. Angeline Scott was off-limits. She always had been. He was old enough and wise enough now not to ignore that crucial fact. Angeline had no hope of a reconciliation with her father if R.J. reentered her life. He couldn't do that to her twice.

"So now what?" she asked, her head tilted back.

He stole a look at his watch. "Well, now I don't have time to run to my office before my first meeting anyway. So we may as well eat. I'm starved. Can I buy you breakfast?"

She clapped her hands to her legs and rose off the tub. "The least I could do is whip you up some breakfast."

R.J. couldn't clamp down on a grimace. In response, her face twisted into an expression of comical hurt.

"I appreciate the offer, Princess, but if I remember correctly, your culinary skills, particularly when it came to breakfasts, weren't exactly polished."

"But that's just not so anymore. I can prepare a lot of stuff. In fact, I managed to acquire a recipe for some mouthwatering apricot scones. It's one of the recipes printed on my packages. I made some the other day, and there're a few left. And I've got some ginger cake left over that goes great with jasmine tea. It'll take no time to throw it together."

He turned to fully face her again and leaned his hip on the sink behind him. "I don't know how to tell you this, sweetheart, but I was thinking more along the lines of home fries, scrambled eggs with bacon, and thick country toast soaked in butter."

She wrinkled her nose. "Those hardly work well with even the briskest of teas."

"And a strong cup of steamy, dark-as-coal coffee."

Angel let out an exaggerated gasp and clapped a palm to her chest. "I can't believe you said the *C* word."

He grinned. "Real bastard, aren't I?"

"I suppose I should go see if I even have a stash of that contraband on the premises."

"Hey, you offered breakfast. If that means you take a walk to Java Jay's, then I'll see you when you get back."

"More forbidden words." She performed an exaggerated shudder. "I can't be around you any longer."

"Sorry, sweetheart. I was never much of a tea drinker."

"Well, you needn't goad me with the competition."

"Would you rather I lied to you?"

"Only if you do it with sincerity." She brushed by him with an exaggerated huff. He snapped her playfully with a towel as she walked out.

Minutes later, the delicious aroma of coffee reached his nostrils, followed by the scent of clearly greasy breakfast home fries. His stomach grumbled. Oh, yeah, it appeared his wife had undergone quite a few changes.

The scene that greeted him in the country-style contemporary kitchen caused an ache deep within his chest. Angel stood over the granite counter, still wrapped in the thick terry robe, fixing breakfast for the two of them. Her collar had fallen off her shoulder. For a moment, he imagined it slipping farther down, lower and lower, exposing the creamy skin of her smooth back. He took a deep breath and made his way to the round wood table in the center of the room.

She turned and acknowledged him with a smile that didn't look very convincing. The events of the morning hadn't been forgotten.

"Voila." She bowed and lifted the cover off a large serving plate to display a heaping serving of eggs, toast and potatoes.

"You did this?"

She glared at him. "I am in the business, sir. You needn't look so surprised."

He figured it would be safer to dig in than risk further reply. He sank his fork into a mound of eggs and barely allowed himself a chew before he swallowed. Early-morning deception tended to give a guy an appetite.

"Mmm, that's great, Angel."

"Glad you like it." She leaned over the table to serve herself. His gaze shifted automatically to her exposed shoulder. She looked up in time to catch his stare and shifted uncomfortably. Slightly embarrassed, he looked away.

He gulped down some of the coffee. It wasn't

terribly fresh, but the caffeine jolt was more than welcome.

Angel lifted her hand, and he handed her the salt shaker before she had a chance to ask for it. She took it without looking up.

"R.J., what in the world do we do now?"

"First of all, I guess we need to set up our trip," he said, stalling. "I understand it's a very pretty area."

"Um..." Angel replied, still chewing. "Especially closer to the Black Sea coast where the Bays' property is." She smiled. "You should see how beautiful these rows and rows of plants are. Mila's Bloom is a gorgeous shrub. It grows so lush and full. There are some black tea orchards right around that area, too. And the beaches are beautiful."

"Well, I'll be able to see it firsthand soon."

She set her fork down. "So, we're really going to go through with this. I guess that European expansion is a lot more important to your bottom line than I had thought." She put her fork down and waited for him to answer.

He ignored it. "Then we can see about the flight arrangements."

"What about your responsibilities? Are you going to be able to get away for so long?"

"I have a right-hand man. I can trust him with my life." He stopped and added, "And with my business."

"Sounds like quite a guy. Can't wait to meet him."

There was no need to tell her Tom already knew about her. No need to talk about the reckless, drunken rant he'd gone on one night when he'd been particularly missing her. He cleared his throat.

"What about you—who'll take over for you here?"

She swallowed. "Shanna's more than capable of handling things while I'm away. And she loves having Max stay with her, so she'll do that, too."

"You two make quite a team."

"We do seem to complement each other." She smiled and picked further at her plate. "Well, our backup in the States seems settled."

He stopped eating. "That's it, then. Looks like we'll be going undercover."

As true man and wife, no less.

CHAPTER FIVE

WHEN IT CAME to late-night wallowing, Shanna Martin always came prepared. Evidence of the fact sat scattered all over the coffee table in the form of candy, ice cream and various other sugar products.

Shifting her legs under her, Angeline tore open the chocolate-covered almonds and popped three of them into her mouth at once. A nearly empty pizza box sat precariously on the arm of the sofa next to her.

"So, you and R.J. will be playing house for a while, huh?"

She started to deny Shanna's depiction but then sighed. "Pretty much." It took an amazingly short time to suck right through the chocolate candy straight to the nut at the center.

"How are you going to make sure the Bays don't become suspicious?" Shanna asked as she stirred her root beer float.

"Shan, I don't know anything anymore. How

did this get so convoluted? It was supposed to be one night of playacting until we could get the Bays to listen to reason."

"Instead, you're traveling in a few days to one of the most romantic spots on the planet with your estranged husband."

"Exactly! How did all this happen?"

Shanna looked like she was on the verge of a giggle, then had the sense to squelch it.

"My life seems to turn completely upside down every time that man is in it." Angeline stopped to wash down two chocolates with cola.

"So now what?"

"So now it's happening all over again. So much for our well-thought-out foolproof plan. We should have been over with this whole thing by now."

"Is that what bothers you? The fact that we're way off plan?"

Angel swallowed and gave her a quizzical look.

"Or is it something else?" Shanna asked while taking great effort in squeezing just the right amount of chocolate syrup onto a pint of French vanilla ice cream. Then she handed the sundae to Angel.

"Isn't that enough?"

"There seems to be more to it. You look almost

angry. Surely not at R.J. He's being very generous. What's going on?"

"Oh, he's generous to a fault. Doesn't seemed
bothered at all that we'll be spending so much
time together."

"Mmm-hmm."

Her blood sugar having reached full tilt, Angel
wasn't cautious enough not to take the bait. "What
do you mean, *mmm-hmm*?"

"I mean, there's something else bugging you
about this whole thing."

"What are you talking about? We're mislead-
ing two wonderful people to help grow a business
that employs numerous hardworking, deserving
women. Not to mention the whole fiasco of a sham
marriage. All of that is bugging me."

"Right." Shanna put her drink down and turned
to face her friend. Uncomfortable with the scru-
tiny, Angel studied the smeared fudge on her
spoon. "But, you're definitely not the objective,
savvy businesswoman you usually are, Angel.
Tell me what's up."

She blurted it out without really wanting to. "It
just hurts, Shan. To see how unaffected he can be
about the whole thing. He acts like it's not going to
bother him at all, pretending we never broke up."

"Like you're wondering how much the marriage meant to him in the first place."

Feeling the tears pool beneath her lids, she could only nod.

Shanna moved closer and gave her a reassuring hug. "Baby, you know he cares for you, he loved you."

"I don't know anything of the sort. Maybe he only loved the fact that I was willing to risk everything for him."

"You don't believe that. Anyone who saw the two of you together could see the intensity whenever you even looked at each other."

"Yeah, the intensity of foolish youth thrown together with a healthy helping of ordinary, basic lust."

"I know you don't want to minimize it that way. Everyone could tell back then that no one else existed for the two of you when you were together."

Angel hmphed a laugh. "That didn't stop several people from trying to come between us. They ultimately succeeded, didn't they?"

"Did they?"

"You need to ask? We split up, remember?"

"Angeline, the only people who can split a couple up are the two people in it."

Angeline paused as the force of each word hammered home. It was true. Somehow she had failed miserably with the one man she'd ever felt anything for.

"You never talked about it, you know," Shanna continued. "You never talked about the specifics of your breakup, I mean." She paused. "And I didn't want to push."

It was true. Shanna was one of those friends who would never prod, just always be there to listen if you needed. It was one of the many reasons they'd stayed such steadfast girlfriends since childhood. Angeline gave a small shrug. "We just grew apart."

"But why?"

"I don't know, we just argued about everything. And the last straw broke when he wanted to move to the West Coast, to be closer to the tech industry. I couldn't drop everything I was doing and follow him to another city." She felt her lip quiver and hated herself for it.

"You were his wife. Couldn't you two work out some sort of compromise?"

"How? I had an idea and a business plan. I'd already put in a large investment."

"And R.J. had a problem with this?"

"He wanted me to look into setting up my business out there. But that was just too risky. Besides, this is my home. R.J., on the other hand, wanted to completely break free from all our Boston connections."

"Doesn't sound like either of you was willing to budge."

Angeline sighed. "It was a very difficult situation, Shanna. I was trying to start my own business."

"Angeline, lots of couples go through what you described. Not all of them end up in splitting. So why did you two break up?"

Angeline snapped her head up to look at her. Random thoughts skittered around her brain like insects. There seemed to have been so many things that went wrong before all that, so many disagreements that escalated. Eventually, even the fire of passion hadn't been enough to keep them together. And there was always the looming specter of her father and his disapproval. She'd initially thought they'd be able to survive it all. Toward the end, she'd realized she didn't even know if she was fighting for her marriage or fighting against her dad. Eye-opening moment, indeed.

"It certainly didn't help that my father was

against us from the beginning. Threatened to cut me off if I married R.J. Then held true to his word. As always."

"You married him anyway."

"I'd fallen in love," Angeline said, grabbing another candy, then slamming it back down on the counter. Suddenly, she didn't feel like eating anymore. "And it's not like my father and I had much of a relationship in the first place. Hence, all the hours I spent at your house as a kid."

Shanna smiled. "We were happy to have you."

"I'm glad someone was. My father treated me as barely more than a nuisance. Something changed in him after my mother left us. He grew cold, distant. I was little, but I still noticed."

"You look a lot like your mom."

She had considered that, of course. "A reminder of her he didn't want." She shook her head in dismissal. "This is all old news. Nothing to do with what's happening between R.J. and me now."

"Maybe. Maybe not. Did it ever occur to you that R.J. may have felt guilty? For coming between you and your father? The only family you had?"

Her pulse hitched. The truth was, she hadn't really examined R.J.'s motivation. She'd been too hurt. But that theory made no sense. "So his response was to give me an ultimatum about moving away with him to the West Coast?"

Shanna leaned closer, her head practically on Angeline's shoulder. "Maybe he knew you well enough to know you'd turn it down. Leaving the ultimate decision in your hands."

Shanna's words felt like a jolt through her chest. Could that have actually been R.J.'s intent? All this time, she hadn't once considered he might have made his West Coast ultimatum in order to give her a way out.

Shanna gave her a look of sympathetic understanding at her silent answer. "That's what I thought," she finally said. "Neither of you stopped to consider what you were really throwing away. Pride and youth kept getting in the way, I imagine."

She watched as Shanna started clearing the mass of junk food in front of them. Had she been uncompromising? She thought back to the woman she was three years ago. Starting and expanding TeaLC had been the ultimate goal. It had been thrilling to investigate the growing tea market, to research the best distribution channels. She'd worked so hard. Sacrificed so much. While her friends were traveling the world after graduating or immersing themselves in social functions, she was poring over project charts and earnings projections. She'd given up so much, her youth, her friends. Her husband. Had it all been worth it in the end? These days, the only thing exciting about TeaLC appeared to be the Works program.

Had she really not stopped long enough to see what her husband was dealing with because he'd married her?

She pulled herself short. Why was she doubting herself all of a sudden? For doing nothing more than pursuing a dream. He'd been at fault, too. If Shanna was right about R.J.'s intentions three years ago, he should have been honest with her from the beginning.

Shanna made a studious effort of studying her scarlet-red fingernail. "Apparently nothing was resolved by the two of you breaking up. You're going to have to address that, even if this is only a short-term 'marriage of convenience.'"

Angel had to stop herself from jumping up and pacing around the living room like a nervous cat.

Shanna continued. "Who knows, maybe that's the reason all this is happening. Maybe the universe is finally answering your need to face some of this stuff head-on. Before you finally move ahead and sign those divorce papers."

Angeline began clearing the table, as well. "Don't you go into one of your New Age, karma-based, transcendental philosophical lectures on me. All this is happening because I'm trying to buy tea from the two sweetest but most stubborn people on the face of the earth."

Shanna threw a chocolate drop at her. "If you say so. But something tells me there's much more to it."

Angel spread her arms wide in a frustrated gesture. "Oh, like what? Perhaps fate has chosen this way to bring us together again? Come on, Shan. Even you can't believe that, romantic that you are."

Shanna shook a spoon in the air. "Don't be so sure. We romantics believe in love above all."

"Despite all the horrors we see at the TeaLC Works program? All those women who commit to the man of their dreams and end up with a nightmare instead?"

"Those women are moving on with their lives. They'll find real love, too. Eventually."

Angeline gave a weary sigh. "And us?"

"Darling, there's only one of us who hasn't had

it happen to her yet. And my turn is right around the corner. I can feel it."

Angel ignored the first part and grinned. "Whoever he is, he's a lucky man."

Shanna winked. "Well, I'll be sure and tell him that when he shows up. Now, I should get going and you should go to bed. We have a pretty full day tomorrow. Don't forget you have that formal dinner in the evening with the Women in International Business."

Angel tried to rub some tension out of her brow. "That's right. I'm not so sure how social I'm going to be. I can just see the conversations now—'Angeline, why don't you tell us about your current overseas projects?' How would I reply?" She placed her hands on her hips and looked up at the ceiling as she thought of a mock answer. "Well, I'm in phase three of 'Operation Marriage Scam.'"

Shanna laughed. "Don't go giving away all our trade secrets."

"And I suppose, before the day is out, I should call R.J. about our trip."

"Looks like you've got a pretty interesting day ahead of you."

Angeline dropped herself back down on the

sofa. "That's the problem. Things have just gotten way too interesting since my ex returned."

Angel stepped out of the double doors of the World Trade Center. Cool harbor wind licked her face and offered some refreshing air. The business dinner had been a chore. She hadn't been able to concentrate. All she could think of was the trip.

She still hadn't called R.J. to talk, had put if off all day. She looked down at her watch. Seven thirty. A walk would soothe her tension. She could grab a cab right afterward and then call him. The wind was crisp and she was wearing heels, but the air would do her good.

Pulling her wrap tighter around her exposed shoulders, she moved down the steps. In the distance to her right, the flickering lights of the city twinkled against the skyline. From the harbor behind her came the unmistakable aroma of low tide.

She turned and started walking toward the city. The building that housed her TeaLC's headquarters stood west of center. It loomed before her like a symbol of her life. She thought about what she was ready to do for the business that building housed, the trip she was about to take and the underlying deception behind it. But she had to. She couldn't let any of her employees lose their jobs.

R.J. was willing to do so much to help her. But that was just his nature. She couldn't take it to mean he still cared for her. That would be a mistake, one too costly for her heart to handle. By all logical conclusions, he had moved on. For all she knew, there was probably even a woman in his life right now.

And what about all the things Shanna had brought up last night? Had R.J. indeed left because he'd made the misplaced assumption that she'd be better off?

Did she dare confront him about it?

She hadn't been able to admit it to her best friend, but the simple fact was that Angel had fully expected R.J. to come back. Maybe in a few months. Perhaps even up to a year. She'd told herself it was just a matter of time before he returned to her.

But he hadn't.

The sudden blare of a car horn sounded as a motorist cut off a van in traffic. The noise brought her attention to her surroundings. She hadn't realized she'd gotten so far. She'd passed the aquarium and all the construction around it without even realizing. Her watch told her she'd been inadvertently walking for almost fifteen minutes.

The hustle of downtown Boston buzzed around her. She tilted her head back to stare at the building before her. Somehow she'd ended up at the last place she wanted to be.

Only one thing left to do now.

R.J. glanced at his watch, then looked back up at her. "What are you doing here, Angel? Did your chauffeur take a wrong turn?"

"I was hoping we could talk."

He lifted an eyebrow. Angeline stood still, braced on the doorway of his hotel suite, afraid to move. The pain in her calf from the long walk in high heels had her lifting her leg to rub it gently. She looked up to see heat swimming in his eyes. He turned away quickly, leaving her to wonder if she'd imagined it.

She straightened. "Can I come in?"

He let out a breath before stepping aside and motioning her inside.

She moved into the room and took a breath for courage. R.J. had the lights dimmed. A large picture window overlooked the city. Rich mahogany furniture adorned the room along with a plush sofa and love seat. It was quite a leap from the one-bedroom studio they had shared as man and wife. That place had only the bare essentials. But R.J. had refused any assistance, including the use of her trust fund. And this was worlds different from the dingy studio over the North End bar where he'd lived during college. She knew it took a rare person to go from a place like that to surroundings like this. Not to mention, this was just one of the properties that R.J. owned. He had real estate holdings all along both coasts.

"I wanted to give you one more chance to change your mind," she began. "I mean, about coming with me."

"I made my decision that morning, Angel. You don't have to worry about me pulling out at the last minute."

She felt some of the tension leave her shoulders. Deep down, she'd known he wasn't going to change his mind. But she had to offer him the out.

"I'd say you're the one who might be having doubts."

She shook her head. "No, I haven't changed my mind."

"You're certain?"

How could she be certain of anything when he

looked at her like that? The warm glow of the dimmed lights threw shadows over his face. His eyes were piercing, intense. His undone collar exposed a triangle of bronze skin and dark chest hair she longed to run fingers over. A small shudder escaped through her, and she hoped he didn't notice.

"I'm certain we've both gone mad." She tried to laugh. "But I know what I have to do. And I appreciate your willingness to help."

"No sweat." He shrugged and walked over to the bar in the corner of the room. "Can I get you anything? Something to drink?"

The last thing she needed in his presence was a drink. Any drop in her inhibitions and she'd be likely to go to him, to touch him the way she'd done the other night when he'd pushed her away.

"No, thank you. I—I just wanted to see you, you know, to be certain."

He nodded and thoroughly looked her over. She tried not to shift uncomfortably under his stare. Suddenly, the low-cut style of her dress, though tasteful, left her feeling exposed. She fought the urge to shift the velvet wrap higher to cover herself. Everywhere his eyes touched felt like steamy water running over her skin.

She cleared her throat. "Perhaps you can answer a question for me, though."

He took another large gulp of his drink and seemed to be in a hurry to swallow it down. "Shoot."

"Why are you willing to do all this? To drop everything and travel across the world with me?"

He only shrugged in answer.

"I know it took a lot of hard work and dedication to get where you are," she continued. "Something tells me that if you want an overseas expansion, you'll find a way to get it yourself."

He looked surprised at her comment. "Thank you for that," he said quietly.

"Which leads me back to my question. Why?"

He shrugged again. "You asked for my help."

She wanted to press it, but there was a warning in his eyes that stopped her. She couldn't name it, but it looked fierce and unforgiving.

"Now I have a question for you," he declared.

"All right."

"Why are you really here?" He stepped away from the bar, slowly, his drink still in his hand. "Dressed like that?"

The shadows in the room seemed to grow suddenly darker. "I told you. I—um—came by to give you one more chance to back out."

"You couldn't have done that with a phone call?" He lifted the glass back to his mouth, his gaze never leaving her face. She watched his lips part and subconsciously opened her own.

She ignored the question. "As for my dress, I had to go to a formal dinner meeting at the pier."

He didn't say anything for a while, just stared at her with an expression that made it clear he wasn't buying it. Why had she shown up here? She'd fully intended to call him.

She cleared her throat. "Well, I should go. I see now I've interrupted you while you were working."

"It can wait." He moved closer, bringing the scent of his distinctive cologne with him. "Right now I'm more interested in getting to the bottom of this."

"Bottom of what?"

"Your visit."

She felt a stinging warmth on her skin, not sure if it was embarrassment or something else. "I—I already told you. What else do you want to hear?"

"I want to know the real reason you're here.

Standing in my living room, in a dress that seems to have been created to reduce a man to tears."

He stared at her as she stood immobile. Angel watched as his eyes traveled over her shoulders, lingering at her chest. A curl of heat meandered its way through her center.

"Is it as smooth as it looks?" he asked in a whisper.

She heard herself gasp. "Wh-what?"

He took large steps toward her. Close, so close. "The dress. Is the velvet as smooth as it looks?" She froze as his hand came up to touch her. He ran a finger over the low collar of the dress, moving provocatively toward the center, where it dipped lower between her breasts. She tried not to react, even as her breathing grew heavier.

She strained for a casual laugh that came out more like a nervous cackle. "Come on, R.J., you think there was some ulterior motive to my coming here like this?"

She tried to step away, but he moved to block her. She could feel his heat over her skin. She tried not to breathe. One deep breath and her chest would come in agonizing contact with his.

"You explain it to me, then, Angel," he challenged. "Tell me why you're here to ask me something you could have asked on the phone. Wearing that."

"It's just a dress, R.J. Nothing more."

He lifted his eyebrows. "Oh, it's so much more. Let me ask you something. Was it the dress you were intending to wear all along to your business dinner? Or was it a spur-of-the-moment decision?"

She tried not to gasp in acknowledged surprise. It had been a last-minute decision. Subconscious, but last minute.

It was time to bring out the defensive artillery. "Aren't you flattering yourself just a little?" God, she hoped she sounded convincing. "I came here to merely talk to you, to make some sort of agreement that we're both fully committed to this trip. Now that I've done that, I think I'll leave."

"And that's it? That's the only reason you're here right now?" He paused as his eyes made another slow, discomforting journey over her.

She cleared her throat. "R.J., you're being silly."

"Am I? Am I being silly when I read desire in your face? I know that desire, Angel. I'm the last man on earth who would mistake that look in your eyes."

She swallowed. "There is no 'look.' I'm stressed

out and I'm tired. My shoes were killing me the whole way here." She stared at him defiantly, trying to quell the effect his closeness was having on her. "Exhaustion. That's what you're seeing. Nothing more than pure physical exhaustion."

He gave her a look that clearly said, *The lady doth protest too much.* "You walked here?"

"I needed the air." She could use a large swallow of it now.

"That's a long distance for heels."

"You're not telling me anything my feet don't know."

A knowing look settled across his face. "So you felt the need to walk, in the dark, to offer an apology that could have been delivered on the phone."

"Like I said, I needed some air. It did me a lot of good. It's just too bad my feet didn't agree with the decision."

He bent down then, quickly and unexpectedly. She tried not to jump as warm strong fingers wrapped around her ankle.

Images flashed through her mind, and all she wanted to do was join him down there. On the carpet, feeling the weight of his body on hers. She yanked her foot back with too much force and nearly toppled over backward. "R.J., please don't, I'm fine."

He didn't come up from his crouched position. "Your feet are starting to swell, and your right heel is loose."

Now things were getting romantic, Angel thought drily. It was hard to determine whether to laugh or cry at her predicament. Or should she just give in and ask for what she wanted...?

She gave her head a quick shake. "I—I'll be fine. We'll talk tomorrow. Sorry to have disturbed you."

"We're not finished yet."

As far as she was concerned they were. She twirled around to make a dash to the door, away from the danger of this conversation.

"Angel, just hold on." His voice had grown more gentle, but it was still a demand. "Don't you think you owe me an explanation?"

The last question broke her control. How could he ever expect her to explain this senseless attraction that seemed to consume her? Clutching her purse to her middle like a protective shield, she tried to suck in a calming breath. "I shouldn't have come here. This whole thing is going to be difficult enough. Let's just see how we can best get through the next couple of days and this trip. We don't need to rehash the fires of old attraction."

"If you really meant that, you wouldn't be here, sweetheart."

"I told you, I realize now that I shouldn't have come."

"But you did."

She felt tears of frustration and swore they would not fall. "Why are you doing this?"

He moved quickly, so fast she could have sworn she felt the air move around her. She felt herself being pulled up against him. "I agreed to become involved because I assumed you were being straight with me. You said you needed help with a small business matter and that only I fit the job requirement. If there's more between us than that, I need to know about it."

"I don't know why you're so worked up over a simple visit."

He gently but effectively pushed her up against the wall, then followed to lean up against her. It was sweet agony to feel his weight against her again, to have his heat on her skin.

"Let's just call it precaution, darling."

She wanted to fling her anger at him, wanted to wound him with harsh words and strong denials. She wanted to scream that there was nothing between them. But the lies wouldn't form on her tongue. Instead, the truth started to roll out. "Do you want me to admit it? Is that it? Do you want to hear that I still yearn for you, that I've missed your touch every day since you left?" Thoroughly disgusted with herself at the complete lack of control, she tried to quell the shaking.

"Is that what you want from me?"

R.J.'s eyes grew wide. Then instantaneously turned darker.

"What did you just say?" His lips were so tight and his voice so low that she almost wondered if she'd imagined the words.

Suddenly it was all too much: the pressure of the last few days, the threat of losing her business. Confronting her dangerous attraction to a man she should have forgotten long ago. Afraid to stay in his presence a moment longer, she yanked herself out of his grasp and ran to the door.

"Angel, wait."

"No. I'm leaving now, R.J." A rock had appeared right above her throat. It was painful and choking.

"Don't. Not yet, please. Not like this."

She wasn't listening anymore. Everything she

did in his presence seemed to take a wrong turn. Her vision blurred as her eyes began to sting. All that mattered now was to leave his apartment as soon as possible. She gripped the doorknob so tight her hand hurt.

"Angel, I didn't mean to be so hard on you. You—you just threw me off."

She had thrown *him* off? Her life had become an out-of-control ride on a speedy Tilt-A-Whirl since he'd shown up in her office a few days ago.

"I'm sorry I keep disrupting your life," she said over her shoulder. "Once this is over, it will never happen again." The last word came out on a sob, and she despised herself for it. How pathetic could she be?

"That's not what I meant. For God's sake, would you just hang on?"

She couldn't. She yanked the door open. The hallway swam in front of her, and she started to run as she felt him closing in behind her.

"Angel, please. Give me another second."

"R.J., not now!" she said, afraid to turn around. She ran past the elevator, not wanting to wait.

"Sweetheart, I'm sorry I snapped. Would you just wait—?"

She hurried down the hallway, cursing herself

as a coward. But for all her successes and all her accomplishments, she didn't have the strength to face the man behind her.

The loose heel of her shoe wobbled, but she ignored it. She was almost at the stairway. The only important thing right now was to get out of here.

She reached the emergency stairs and yanked open the door, R.J. hard on her heels.

"Damn it, Angel. You're going to tumble down those steps. Would you please just stop?" He was near pleading now, the urgency thick in his voice.

But she couldn't stop. She couldn't even slow down.

"Angel, I'm not going to follow you. All right? Just slow down before you hurt yourself."

She didn't heed him. Her heel gave another twist, and she inadvertently took two steps at a time. Her foot landed on the hard stone and shot a jolt of pain through her already sensitive ankle. She stumbled but managed to right herself. R.J.'s gasp was audible from behind her, even though it was obvious he wasn't pursuing her any longer.

She saw the exit sign and hiccupped with relief. Just a few more steps. When she pushed the door open, cool air finally hit her like a smooth, satin curtain. She stopped on the sidewalk to catch her breath.

"Angel, please," she heard him say behind her several moments later.

How could she let him see her cry this way? It was bad enough he'd read her so well, bad enough he had figured it out before she could even admit it to herself. No, she had to get away from him. She ran to the curb, desperate to find a taxi.

Her heel finally gave way. She felt herself plunging toward the ground and braced for the inevitable pain of impact with the hard concrete. Before she could even cry out, strong arms gripped her at the waist and stopped her fall.

It took a moment to regain her breath, then she said the first words that came into her head. "Nice catch."

He remained silent for a beat. "Yeah, you were."

God, it felt right. Being in his arms felt like being home. All she could think about was the feel of him.

"I—I guess I totally lost that heel."

"You lost the whole shoe."

Despite herself, she let out a small laugh.

She moved to disengage herself, and he shook his head. "Uh-uh. You can't walk like that."

What was the alternative? Suddenly, he picked her up and turned around back toward his building. She didn't protest. Her husband was carrying her back to his hotel room in the middle of the night. And she wasn't going to protest.

Strangers stared at them, but she hardly noticed. The old sensation that they were the only souls on earth manifested itself like habit. She gave in to the urge to snuggle into his chest.

They seemed to be moving in slow motion through the stairway.

"I'm sorry."

She looked up and brought shaky fingers to his lips.

"Don't. Please don't apologize."

"I need to. I don't know what came over me. But you showed up, and you looked so damn—" He let out a frustrated breath. "So much like the way I remembered. And it—"

Intuitively, she knew they had both moved toward each other.

Anticipation froze her muscles. Nothing moved but her heart. Even time seemed to stop.

He pulled back from her suddenly, a quiet moan on his lips.

"Angel?"

"Yes?"

"I'm taking you back upstairs."

CHAPTER SIX

HE INTOXICATED HER. Why else would she be allowing this to happen? Savoring it?

She was still cradled in his arms when they stepped back into his hotel suite. He dropped his forehead on hers and slowly started to lower her to the floor. She clutched at his shoulders, savoring his heat as she traveled down the length of him.

This was the way it had always been between them, so much fire it was a wonder their souls hadn't scorched. He nuzzled against her as he settled her onto her feet, and she thought she'd never realized such pleasure.

Until he set her down and a shooting pain shot through her calf. Angel gasped.

"Don't tell me—your foot?" R.J. said above her.

She nodded, clenching her teeth against the hurt.

"Here, sit down." He gently maneuvered her onto the sofa. "Let me take a look. I've had quite a few injuries in my lifetime." Angel knew the reasons for that. R.J. had grown up on some of the toughest streets of metro Boston. He'd been in more than his fair share of fights, an aspect of his life he refused to talk about. She could hardly blame him. He softly touched her ankle with gentle fingers.

"It's swollen even more, but it doesn't appear sprained." He wrapped his hand around the top of her foot, applying gentle pressure. The innocent massage sent fire up her leg. Full-blown kisses from other men had elicited less desire.

"R.J., you don't have to do this."

"I just want to reduce the swelling." He continued to massage her ankle. "I'll have the bellboy bring up an ice pack in a minute."

She tried not to imagine his hand moving higher, his palm slowly moving over her calf, around her knee, up toward her thigh.

She couldn't stand it anymore.

She braced her hands at his shoulders to stop him. "R.J., really. Don't. I don't need an ice pack either."

He looked up at her, then his gaze dropped first to where her right hand was on his shoulder. Then followed it to her left hand. She realized how tightly she was squeezing him.

She hadn't meant to grab him so intimately. But it was impossible to move, to let go.

He reached up and gently touched her cheek. "It's okay," he whispered.

She felt her lips part, felt herself move closer to him. It felt so easy, so natural. "R.J., I—I've really missed you."

A sad smile formed on his lips. "Me, too, Princess. Me, too."

"It's been such a long time."

"I know." His thumb moved on her cheek. "I didn't think I'd ever see you. Let alone be made to act like your loving husband again."

They both stilled at the words. Hearing the actual term seemed to drive home the enormity of what they were about to do. To actually travel overseas together where they would pretend they'd never even separated.

R.J. stood suddenly. "We have quite a few days ahead of us, don't we?"

Such an understatement. What in heaven's name was she doing? Why was she letting her attraction rule her again? Their circumstances were complicated enough. She shouldn't be here. She shouldn't be admitting to having feelings for him.

R.J. had his head tilted back, his eyes shut. He looked utterly drained.

Reality had hit them both.

She cleared her throat. Did he realize how difficult it was going to be traveling with him, pretending to be his woman? All the while knowing that none of it meant anything. Not to him.

"I'm not sure I'll be able to act the part," she admitted.

R.J.'s lips pursed into a tight line. When he looked back down at her, all hint of gentleness had left his eyes.

"I'll call you a taxi," he declared. "Try to stay off that ankle until the swelling goes down."

"I—I will," she answered, faltering at the sudden change in him.

"I'll instruct the bellboy to come help you when the cab arrives. Now, if you'll excuse me, I realize I do have a lot of work to do."

She watched dumbfounded as he walked away. It was regret. He was angry for letting himself come so close to her again. Well, so be it. It was fine with her if he wanted her to leave.

He turned back to her suddenly, and she nearly jumped. "Oh, and Angel?"

"Yes?"

"I'm sorry I lost myself a minute ago. I won't let things go this far again."

She bit down on her lip, anger completely numbing any pain she may have felt in her foot. She gave him a stiff nod in response.

What did she expect? She was twenty-seven years old and still hadn't learned to manage her overzealous hormones when it came to her ex-husband. Dressing up for him, albeit unintentionally, taunting him. She had to get a handle on her attraction. Before it was too late.

His next words just drove it home. "Do me a favor and don't pack that dress."

R.J. watched from his window as the bellboy assisted Angeline into her cab. He cursed himself as the car pulled away from the curb and drove into traffic.

He'd almost lost control. And the pretending hadn't even started yet.

I'm not sure I'll be able to act the part.

How could he have been so stupid? That's all this was supposed to be—the two of them acting, for a business deal. He'd almost lost himself again. Just because she'd worn that dress. First he'd lashed out at her, then he'd been ready to ravish her right there on the sofa. He'd spent years disciplining himself, working toward his goals. Now he couldn't contain himself because of a damn dress.

Her father's words echoed in his head. *"I hope you're smart enough to stay away from her. Sign those damn divorce papers already. So she can move on to someone more suitable."*

R.J. gripped his glass tighter in his hand. To think, for a split second upon accidently running into him, R.J. had thought that maybe Richard Scott was cornering him to make peace. Perhaps he would even commend him on how far R.J. had come since he'd become his son-in-law.

Foolish. Why had he expected anything like acceptance from a man like Richard Scott when his very own father had never given him anything of the kind? Why had R.J. expected anything but scorn?

And why had he expected it of the man who'd once even tried to bribe him out of his daughter's life?

R.J. walked over to the bar and slammed his glass down. What remained of his drink splashed over the side onto the rich glossy wood. She was right. This was simply a part he'd be playing.

Then he'd remove himself from her life for good. Or Angeline would never have a chance to reconcile with her father.

This wasn't going to be a reunion between them. She'd asked for his help, and he was still such a fool for her he'd agreed to give it. Hell, he'd done more than that. He was actually going to travel to the supplier's estate with her. But he had his motives. She'd lost everything because of him; her inheritance, standing, her father.

But there was no excuse for letting Angel get under his skin the way she had tonight. Why had she shown up here? She didn't know what she wanted. In one breath she was talking about how much she'd missed his touch and in the next she was reminding him they were doing nothing but playacting for the sake of her business.

It couldn't be anything more.

Sure, he was no longer the outclassed lowbrow he'd been when they'd first met. But he didn't have the bloodlines her friends and family required. As her father had unequivocally explained at their unexpected meeting, that wasn't something he could work hard to achieve. No matter how hard he tried.

For some unknown reason fate had brought

them together once again. Maybe his life had become too peaceful. Maybe he was becoming too complacent. And some unknown force had said: let's see how you deal with Angeline Scott again all these years later.

R.J. let out a small laugh. That's what it was. This was all a big joke. A joke on him. Well, he wouldn't forget again. He'd remember from now on that they were both only playing a part.

"Angel, wake up."

"Hmm?"

"Wake up, we're landing. Final destination, we're here."

A warm hand gently caressed a path down her cheek, and she turned her face into it. R.J. was touching her. She was snuggled close up against him.

A small sound of pleasure escaped her lips through the caverns of sleep.

"Oh, Lord," she heard a strangled voice say. She moved her lips into the hand that was now cupping her face.

Funny, her dreams had never felt so real before. She didn't want to wake up from this one. A curl of heat slowly kindled inside her rib cage. The harsh jolt of the wheels touching down shocked her awake. Angeline shook the cobwebs out of her head and forced herself to move. Her surroundings slowly started to register.

So it hadn't been a dream.

"I guess I was asleep," she said groggily.

"You say and do some interesting things in your sleep. I'd forgotten."

She was practically sprawled on top of him. "I—I'm sorry." Though it almost hurt to pull back to her own seat, she forced herself.

"For?" he asked.

"For collapsing on top of you like that. I hope I didn't make you too uncomfortable."

He swallowed, tension etched in his face. "Not in the way you think." His words put her at a loss for her own. The plane came to a sudden and jerky stop.

She barely noticed when the speaker above them crackled and then came fully to life. "Ladies and gentlemen, your flight crew welcomes you to Tels, Mondolavia. Please go to your left as you enter the airport. We look forward to serving you again."

R.J. dropped his hand and stood. Moving with his usual efficiency and competence, he pulled their bags from the overhead compartments.

"I guess the adventure begins," he remarked as he stepped aside to let her into the aisle.

"I guess."

After a brief stop at the gate, they made their way to the airport exit. She heard someone shouting for them as they walked outside.

"Angeline, R.J. Welcome, welcome." It was Tavov.

"Tavov!" She felt a genuine smile. "So nice to see you again."

"Yes, same to you." He motioned for them to follow him to a waiting car at the corner.

Angeline slowly took in her surroundings. The sun appeared bright in the sky, but the temperature outside was comfortably warm. Lush hills surrounded the airport. The air smelled faintly of the sea.

A comfortable silence filled the space of the luxury vehicle when they started the drive. The road curved around hills and cliffs. In the distance, the water gleamed. Finally, they turned onto the small road that lead to the Bay's estate. A large iron gate came into view. Tavov waited at the entrance while a man in tan overalls ran out to let them in. He tipped his head in greeting as they drove past.

With all the stress over securing the deal, she'd nearly forgotten how lovely the Bay's property was. The large white house with pillars stood majestically at the end of the road. Angel found herself distracted by the Greek-style mansion and the lush landscape surrounding it. She noticed the brilliant greenery as they all got out of the car. Nowhere else had she seen grass quite that color of jade.

The front door flew open, and Mila stepped outside. Waving, she walked toward them as Tavov and R.J. emptied the trunk of their bags.

"Angeline, R.J. So great to see you again."

"Hello, Mila." Angel accepted the other woman's hug, then watched as she embraced R.J., as well.

"Come, let's get you settled."

They followed Mila through the large foyer. The walls were adorned with colorful Middle Eastern art. Thick silk rugs covered wooden floors.

"We've put you in a suite on the second floor," Mila said over her shoulder as they followed her up a winding staircase.

A suite. R.J. looked over his shoulder at her. They hadn't had a chance to discuss their living arrangements. Of course the Bays would expect them to be comfortable in a one-bedroom suite.

If she had any luck whatsoever, there would be a large couch in addition to the bed.

"This is it." Mila indicated a door on their left. Angel crossed her fingers as the other woman opened the door. They entered a charming, spacious room. Angel took stock of her surroundings. Sliding glass doors leading to a balcony offered a majestic view of the beach and ocean. Two wooden rocking chairs sat on opposite corners, on either side of the glass doors. A large bed with an ornate burgundy cover faced the balcony. There was a colorful silk Turkish rug covering the center of the wooden floor, clearly handmade.

The room was beautiful. But there was no couch. That finger-cross thing never did seem to work.

"Through that door is the washroom." Mila pointed. "And right next to it is the closet."

Angel realized it immediately. R.J.'s expression told her he did, too. Far from being lucky in any way, by some strange stroke of misfortune, the layout of the small suite was uncannily similar to that of their first shared apartment as newlyweds.

* * *

Images flooded her mind. Her eyes darted toward the bed, and the visuals tripled in intensity.

She looked back to find R.J. watching her. A warm flush reached her cheeks. He must have known exactly where her thoughts had drifted. She didn't bother to look away.

"What do you think?" Mila was asking, motioning to the room in general.

"It should do just fine." R.J. smiled, but Angel didn't miss the hardened timbre that had reached his voice.

Angeline turned away from the bed and walked over to the balcony.

"Mila, the view is breathtaking. We'll be more than comfortable. Thank you."

Mila practically beamed in pleasure, apparently taking her responsibility as hostess seriously. "In that case, I'll let the two of you freshen up. Why don't you meet us downstairs for afternoon tea when you're ready?"

Angel watched as Mila shut the door behind her. R.J. had walked over next to her to stare out over the balcony.

"I just can't believe all this." What had she gotten the two of them into?

She removed the elastic holding her ponytail in place. Hard to believe, but she was actually feeling a slight ease in the tenseness of her shoulders. Even given R.J.'s close proximity.

She turned to look at the bed. "I suppose we'd better figure out our sleeping arrangements."

"There's nothing to talk about. I'll find a way to make myself comfortable on the floor."

"That hardly seems possible."

"I've slept in worse conditions. Way worse."

Still, she didn't want him to have to sleep on a hard floor. Especially tonight, following the long trip they'd taken. But what other choice was there?

"R.J., we could take turns. We're in this together, it's only fair. Why don't I sleep on the floor tonight?"

He turned quickly. "I have yet to make a woman uncomfortable while spending the night with me. I don't intend to start with my Brahmin wife."

The sexual innuendo stopped her heart briefly. And exactly how many women fell into that category anyway?

The last thought triggered an angry response. "This may be hard for you to believe, but I have 'roughed it' in the past."

It wasn't a bald-faced lie, although most people's definition of roughing it probably couldn't be held comparable to hers. Still, she'd gone camping, hadn't she? Even if it was in a well-equipped cabin with all the worldly comforts in the luxurious backdrop of the Swiss mountains.

The corner of his mouth lifted. All right, so it was a bald-faced lie.

"Go ahead and laugh," she told him.

He did. And he looked so sexy, so incredibly appealing. Suddenly all she wanted to do was to touch him, to have him hold her.

"Angel, you sleep on the bed. Believe me, the hardness of the floor is the last thing I'll be thinking about tonight."

She didn't have to guess what he meant. This would be the first night in three years they'd been so close together. Only a few feet apart with the sensuous sounds of the ocean drifting into the room. Five days pretending to be really married, together twenty-four hours a day. She shivered slightly. She had to stay focused on the issue here. Getting Mila and Tavov to sign the supply contract and going back to Boston with a clear plan for growth. She could handle a few awkward days to achieve that.

She turned away and made for the bureau chest

behind her. "Well, perhaps we could find you a blanket or something. That throw rug, as beautiful as it is, is not going to do much for your back."

She pictured him sprawled out on the floor asleep and furiously started rummaging through the drawer's contents. There didn't seem to be anything in there besides a thin afghan.

He was behind her all of a sudden and grabbed her hand gently. "I'll be fine on the floor, Angel."

She stilled at the contact and looked up to meet his eyes in the mirror above the chest. The awkwardness of their surroundings hung unspoken between them.

"The room looks so familiar." She wasn't sure she had meant to say it out loud.

"Yeah, it does."

Did it bring back memories for him, too? Memories of the intimate, unguarded moments they'd shared?

"I've thought of that first apartment often," she admitted.

"Some things are better forgotten."

She looked up at him, saw the familiar yet frustrating curtain guarding any emotion in his eyes.

"Perhaps you're right," she said. But there were some things a woman could never forget. That was the apartment he'd carried her into as his wife, and they hadn't left the bedroom until the next afternoon. It was there where they'd talked about all their dreams around the ragged breakfast bar in the center of the kitchen.

But it was also the same apartment where they'd had their harshest arguments.

"It never occurred to me we wouldn't be moving out of there together," she found herself admitting.

He nodded slightly in the mirror above her. "Me neither. But we both made our decisions. Right or wrong."

Would he ever understand? She turned back around and leaned against the bureau. "I guess we'll always disagree on the importance I placed on starting my own business."

The raised eyebrow suddenly fell into a straight line. "Is that what you think?"

She shook her head. He looked away from her, up toward the ceiling.

"I told you how important it was for me to start this business venture, R.J. But all that mattered to you was getting away. You couldn't wait to leave Boston."

He lifted his hand in the air impatiently. "I had

no business in Boston anymore. Not after college. And especially not after we started to grow apart."

"We were still close in a lot of ways when things started to fall apart."

He swallowed. "Being compatible in bed can only take a couple so far, Angel. Every time I moved in your circles, it just made me realize what a mistake—" He stopped midsentence.

She tried to ignore the hurt. *Mistake.* There was that word again. Damn him. What they'd felt for each other had not been a mistake. Ever.

"R.J., I had no circles."

He let out a short laugh. "No? What about all the country club boys? The ones who hovered around you like hornets. The same ones who looked at me like I was dirt every time I had the audacity to touch you, even after we were married? What about all the debutantes who looked at you like you'd lost your head?"

"Those were your friends, too. From the football team and from class."

He laughed at that. "Angel, those so-called friends never treated me as more than a wannabe. But when you were around, instead of shunning me outright, they just ignored me. All of them, except, of course, for Shanna."

"I—I just can't believe that."

He laughed again, a humorless, empty sound. He was mocking her. "Face it, with very rare exception, anyone at all close to you hated that you chose me."

"Well I seem to recall several of the females in my so-called 'circles' flirting shamelessly with you, sometimes right under my nose."

"Yeah?" He stepped closer to her, and all the air seemed to have sucked out of the small room. "Even as they propositioned me they made it clear I shouldn't harbor any delusions of grandeur. But they were just being who they were." Her confusion must have shown on her face because he continued. "At least those women were straight with me, Angel. With them I knew from the beginning exactly where I stood."

"What are you saying? That what you got from me wasn't real? That somehow our marriage wasn't real?"

"I'm not saying a thing. The time to say anything about it all is long gone. We were just too young, and too naive, to get married."

He turned from her suddenly and thrust a hand through his hair. "Listen, this is useless. It's gonna be hard enough staying here in such close quarters. Let's just forget about slamming out the past, okay? In the end, it's simple. Our worlds didn't belong together."

It wasn't okay. How could he say those things, think those things? "You think it was senseless of us to fall in love?"

R.J. started to rub his eyes. "It hardly matters. Why don't we just wipe the slate clean, all right? Starting here, starting now. I promise to do whatever I can to make this easier between us." But she noticed he wasn't answering her.

"We have to act and sound like a true married couple after all," he continued when she was silent.

Sure, like a married couple who held hands, who touched each other affectionately. Who shared the same hopes and dreams. Not to mention shared the same bedroom.

Well, he was wrong about her; she'd tried damn hard to make it work between them.

Hadn't she?

CHAPTER SEVEN

SOMETHING WAS DEFINITELY crawling up her leg.

Angeline shook out her left foot, kicking several blades of long grass in the process.

Whatever it was, it was very persistent. She'd swatted it away several times already. There was barely enough light to study her leg if she wanted to look down and identify her tormentor. She didn't.

"Maybe it wasn't such a good idea to go wanderin', huh, missy?" she admonished herself. *Great.* It was never a good sign when she started talking to herself. But she'd just wanted to get away on her own for a while. Just to clear her head.

The luscious, fragrant bushes of Mila's Bloom had beckoned her, and she'd decided to walk around the orchard. Only problem was, now she was lost. And by herself. The shrubs had grown higher than she remembered, and the house was no longer visible.

Now what?

It felt like she'd been in the fields for hours even if her watch told her it was less than twenty minutes. How long did this shrubbery go on anyway?

She suddenly felt a chill. Even with the full moon above, the evening had suddenly grown inexplicably dark. Like a forgotten room that had been shut off from the rest of the house after its occupant had passed away.

The tickly itch traveling up the back of her knee returned. This time it went clear up to her thigh. Angeline gasped in horror. Who would have thought that she'd had the ability to jump and swat at her leg at the same time? The circus must need some kind of talent like that. If this whole tea business thing didn't work out… She shook her head at the silly thoughts and continued moving.

Something grabbed her.

Panic darkened what little light the moon afforded. Angel struggled to pull herself out of the strong grip that had suddenly gotten hold of her. There was a large, male hand wrapped around her upper arm.

"Calm down, it's just me." The unmistakable voice came from behind her ear.

The hand slowly removed itself, and she hurled

herself around. "What do you think you're doing sneaking up on me like that?"

"I could ask you what you're doing out here wandering alone."

She was going to ignore that question. As well as his patronizing tone. "Jeez, R.J. You nearly scared the logic out of me!"

"Again, I ask what you're doing out here. In the dark, by yourself."

Angeline huffed in frustration. Her heart still thudded with fear. "I just needed some time and some air. To think."

"Didn't look like a stroll. It looked more like you were karate chopping some of the plants."

"Ha, ha. I was just about to make my way back."

He quirked an eyebrow. "Is that so? You weren't lost at all?"

"Most definitely not."

"Right." Skepticism laced his voice. "Were you checking out the crop, making sure it's all still worthy of your investment?"

She sighed, utterly weary now after all the excitement. "Was that a jab? I just want to grow my business, R.J. I'm starting to get tired of trying to justify that to you."

He crooked a finger under her chin. It was an

innocent yet oddly sensual action. Under the evening sky, amid a field of aromatic grass with the sounds of the ocean in the distance. Having him touch her in such circumstances was risky. "Angel, you don't have to explain your determination to me. I know firsthand how powerful that is in you."

"I know you didn't mean that as a compliment, but in the interest of harmony, I'm going to take it as one."

"By all means." He stepped aside and gestured for her to go forward. "So, lead the way."

"Ah…me?"

He nodded at her solemnly. "Yes. You know… because you're absolutely not lost."

"Very funny."

"Will you admit it?"

She waited without answering, tapping her foot.

He finally broke the silence with a laugh. "I knew it."

"Don't get cute with me, Robert James Davet. I'd rather not stay in this grass any longer than I have to."

"It was your decision to come out here, Princess." He rubbed his chin. "Now, admit you were lost or I won't show you the way."

"But there are bugs in here," she hissed.

His only answer was to cross his arms in front of his chest.

"Great," Angel muttered. "I'm in one of the most beautiful parts of the world and instead of enjoying it I'm making myself a late-night snack for a swarm of insects."

"All to break out into the herbal tea market."

She sighed. "It would mean so much more than that. It would mean a huge expansion."

Suddenly, the air grew serious. "Let's assume everything goes smoothly on this trip. You get the deal for the exclusive distribution rights. The expansion goes through, the new tea is an instant phenomenon."

Angel closed her eyes, imagining that very scenario. "And every one of my employees will be secure for the foreseeable future. That's all I'm hoping for."

He nodded. "It does sound great. But then what? There's still a loose end."

"Which is?"

"What are you going to tell the Bays when we finally go through with the divorce?"

The question brought a chill to her insides. Divorce. Finally. Of course, she'd known all along that's where her life was headed. She'd be a divorced woman eventually. She and R.J. had just been too busy to move forward with finalizing and before she knew it, three years had gone by. Still, to hear him say it outright somehow jolted her in a way she didn't want to examine.

She gave a small shrug. "There will be only one thing to say, I suppose."

"And that would be?"

"That despite our furtive attempts, we couldn't find a way to make it work."

At that point, at least, she'd be telling the Bays the truth.

Tavov and Mila appeared to have retired for the evening. R.J. shut the door of the suite quietly behind him. He looked up to find Angel gazing nervously at the bed.

They still hadn't worked out their final sleeping arrangements.

He started to reassure her of his intentions when she suddenly jumped. High.

"Oh my God, it's on my neck!" Angel started desperately swatting at her hair.

"What? What's the matter?"

"It's crawling into my hair." There was a note of sheer terror in her voice.

"What is?"

"I'm sure I don't know." She sounded near hysterical. "I assume it's a bug. A large, hairy, slimy bug! It must have crawled on me in the fields."

"Angel, come here and I'll take a look," he tried to say in his most calm, least amused voice. It wasn't easy.

"Get it out, now, please," she shrieked.

The head of a successful distribution business and here she was hysterical over a small bug. "Angel, sweetheart. Just calm down and let me look. But please try not to make any more noise. You're going to have Mila and Tavov wondering what I'm doing to you in here."

He gently pulled her by the shoulders and turned her around. Lifting her hair up, he tried to peer through the mass of tresses to examine her scalp.

"There's nothing there."

"Don't tell me that! I can feel it."

"I don't see anything," he insisted, trying to reassure her.

"Of course you don't, it's inside my hair." She resumed the frantic swatting.

"Look, just relax. Here, let me." He cupped the

back of her neck, plunging his fingers into her hairline. *Mistake.* He could feel her pulse racing beneath his hand.

"Is it gone?"

It quickly became a struggle to catch his breath. "I don't see or feel anything."

"Please just make sure."

He moved his hand around, trying to ignore the soft, silky feel of her hair across his forearm. A light, citrus scent drifted to his nose. She still used the same shampoo.

She stopped moving, and they both stilled. He had to clear his throat before he could continue. "There's nothing crawling on you, Angel."

"Are you certain?"

Why was it becoming so hard to breathe? "I'm certain," he managed to croak out.

She didn't answer right away, still breathing heavily. "I guess I must have imagined it."

All right, you've checked. Pull your hands off her now. But he couldn't bear to, it was too hard. Her pulse quickened under his palm.

"I guess so." His hand seemed to move on its own. He plunged his fingers farther into the silkiness of her hair and felt her shudder. Soft, she was so soft. Her hair, her skin. His calloused hand felt as if he was running it through a cloud. With zero control, he pulled her closer, her back snug against his chest.

A cricket chirped in the distance, as if to issue a warning cry. He didn't heed it, just gave in as he allowed his lips their slow descent.

She inhaled sharply, and it was all he needed. He tried to bargain with himself, one small kiss, just to see if her skin still held the same warmth. But he knew that was a lie. He had no doubt it would.

He was right. Nothing could have prepared him for the sweet torment that assaulted him as he let his lips fall on the back of her neck. He heard her groan and responded by yanking her closer. Her back was up against him completely. Fire spread through his shirt, then moved lower.

He couldn't stop himself from nuzzling closer into her neck. Even as he cursed himself, he splayed shaky fingers on her abdomen. There was no hiding her effect on him now. She let her head fall back as he moved the kisses around her neck.

He had to stop. But as insane as this was, it felt too right. Besides, he couldn't have stopped if he wanted to. Not when she was leaning into him and uttering those maddeningly erotic sounds under her breath.

She reached behind her and pulled his head closer. His hand moved up, meeting soft, yielding flesh. His fingers burned at the touch of her skin. He started to lower the collar of her dress. He wanted to expose her to him, to run his hands over her breasts, to feel her and taste her like he had so often in the past.

He shouldn't be touching her like this. He shouldn't be wanting her like this. Men like him didn't belong with ladies like Angeline Scott. God, he knew from experience how devastating the results could be of such a foolish union.

Somehow he managed to pull himself away and forced himself to step back. He'd done it again.

Angel turned to look at him and wrapped her arms around herself. "What just happened, R.J.?"

"Something that shouldn't have happened. An error in judgment."

He rubbed a palm across his face and forced himself to calm down, to squash the unwanted urges.

"Well, it did happen, and so did the incident in your apartment back in Boston."

He let out a small laugh. "I guess I need to learn

how to stop making the same mistakes, don't I?" He heard himself echo his father's words.

Angel flinched. "It's not that simple. And I, for one, would like to talk about this."

"I don't think there's anything to talk about."

She spread her arms. "How can you say that? This is the second time we've lost control with each other."

She was right, but there was no point in analyzing something that shouldn't have happened in the first place. "What exactly are we supposed to discuss?"

She squeezed her eyes shut. "Don't you have anything to say?"

"Not really. Except that it won't happen again."

"You're so certain?" she asked. "Can you just turn your feelings off like that? Is it that easy?"

"Easy isn't always—"

"Yeah, I know," she interrupted, impatience laced in her voice. "Easy isn't always better. Well, difficult isn't necessarily right either."

"I suppose with rare exception."

"No, there's nothing rare about it. Why can't you just trust me enough to tell me what you're feeling?"

He took a deep breath. How absurd, to think

he could just say it all to her. To tell her that he'd learned long ago that he couldn't just grab what he wanted. Everything had its price, everything had to be fought for. And sometimes the casualties were too high to risk. Why couldn't she understand that?

"What exactly is it that you want from me?" he asked her.

When she responded, the punch had gone out of her voice. "I just want to know, I guess. To understand. Every time you touch me, it's the way it was. I know you feel it, too. But then you just shut yourself off. How can you do that so well?"

"Angel, it's not too difficult to understand. We both learned the hard way that we're too different. We don't want the same things. You're charities and society balls, I'm South End litter. An intense attraction is not going to change that."

"Are you sure you know me so well?"

"I know what you were born into, the legacy you should be a part of. And I also know how our marriage came between all of that."

"You can't believe any of that matters to me."

"You say that now. How do you know you're not going to wake up one morning and resent that you lost your rightful inheritance because of an impulsive decision you made when you were barely an adult?"

"Falling in love with you was not impulsive. You know," she started. "Shanna said something to me right before this trip."

"What was that?"

"She said the only two people who can break up a relationship are the two people in it."

He knew she was waiting for a response. But suddenly he was just too tired to come up with one.

"Angel, it's late. We're both very tired. Not to mention jet-lagged. We'll talk in the morning."

"No. In the morning you'll just come up with a sugarcoated way to brush everything aside. Just this once, I want you to talk to me instead of pushing me away."

He didn't want this, didn't need to be thinking about all this right now. Her look told him she wasn't in any mood to drop the matter.

"Don't you understand?" he blurted. "We can't forget that people as different as you and me will never really mesh. We're from two completely different worlds."

"And therefore we should have never gotten married? Is that it?" She crossed her arms in front of her chest and shook her head slightly. "What a double standard you have, R.J. Do you have any idea how pompous that would sound coming from, say, someone like me? Someone who grew up with money. What makes you think it's okay for you to come to a conclusion like that?"

"I guess it's one of the few luxuries my background afforded me." He knew his tone held the warmth of a glacier.

"So, just how far do you think such a generality should go?" she pressed.

He shook his head. "What do you mean?"

"Where would you draw the line? Just at marriage? Or any emotional involvement?" What in the world was she getting at?

She stepped up to him, her finger pointed at his chest. "Is it all right to share a purely physical attachment? What if there's no emotional tie? Then is it okay?"

Now they were moving into dangerous territory. Way too dangerous. "What the hell are you talking about? Is what okay?"

She shrugged. "A casual toss in the hay for instance. Is it all right for us to sleep together, as long as that's all we do?"

She'd shocked him. But he recovered quickly.

Before allowing himself to realize what he was about to do, he was in front of her. In an instantaneous movement, he had her by the shoulders and pulled her closer.

"Is that an offer, Angel?"

Suddenly the topic at hand was very different. "I just want to make sure I understand you correctly," she said slowly.

"First let me make sure I understand. Are you offering a no-strings-attached little romp? Something to add to the excitement factor of this trip?"

She started chewing her lip. "I'd like to know exactly where you draw the line between your rules and your feelings."

"Acting on our feelings is what got us into trouble years ago." Even as he said it, he pulled her closer. "We don't want to do it again."

"Why not?" she demanded. "Didn't we agree that the only taboo was any emotional involvement?"

He lowered his head, speaking into her lips. "I'd just like to be clear. Is the respectable and ever so proper Angeline Scott offering her soon-to-be ex-husband a casual fling?"

She swallowed. "It appears so."

"It better be more than appearance, Angel.

You'd better be damn sure you're prepared for me to take you up on it."

"What makes you think I'm not?" As good as she was at bluffing, he knew her too well.

But he wasn't feeling terribly merciful. "What if I call your bluff? Right here. This very moment. Will you still be as sure?"

"You know I'm a woman of my word, R.J."

"I know you used to be."

He kissed her then, a hungry kiss. One meant to take everything and give nothing in return. She responded with longing. She wanted him. He could feel how much.

He stopped finally, shaking with desire. "Well, you've definitely changed. Such a worldly proposition. Apparently you've done some growing up in the last few years."

"I don't see why we can't be adult about this." She cleared her throat, looking him straight in the eye.

"Adult." He smiled, then took his hands off her. It took all his will, but he reluctantly let her go. "Go to bed, Angel." He turned and made his way to the door before he could regret it.

"Wait, where are you going?"

He didn't bother to turn back around. "Out."

* * *

Angel watched the door shut and wanted to throw something at it. Sheer will prevented her from going after him. That and pride. She wasn't going to beg, had come way too close to it just now. She turned and faced the balcony doors. The night had grown dark now, so dark the world beyond the railings appeared to be a limitless empty space.

She'd said she was open to a casual fling. Until the words had left her mouth she wouldn't have believed it. Why had she made such an empty offer? She would have given up so much if R.J. had taken her up on it. She would have given up her heart. The moment he touched her again intimately the already fragile shell around her heart would have crumbled. She knew that was the last thing R.J. wanted.

Why was he trying so hard to deny that he was at least physically attracted to her if nothing else? It didn't matter. He didn't want to get close to her again. So why had she done it?

Silly question. She knew the answer. Because when it came to R.J. she was oh, so ready to take whatever she could get. No matter what the consequences to her pride. He meant that much to her. He always had.

Shanna had been so wrong that night back when they'd indulged in all the junk food. R.J. had left for the West Coast because he'd wanted to. Not to give her an out, not because he'd felt guilty in any way. He'd wanted to move to Silicon Valley, and he was going to do it with or without her. He was an enormously successful businessman now. But he still didn't seem to want their marriage to continue. Just today he'd asked how she was going to break the news of their divorce to the Bays when it happened.

That told her everything she needed to know.

Angel walked over to the balcony doors and pressed her forehead against the glass. She would go crazy if she kept thinking about it, if she kept thinking about him.

Her skin was still on fire, and her breasts felt heavy with the want of his touch. But she would try to ignore all that. As unlikely as it was, she'd try to get some sleep. She'd put her head on the pillow and close her eyes.

And she'd pray that she had the strength to deny her feelings come tomorrow. Deny them as strongly as R.J. insisted on denying his.

* * *

R.J. stepped slowly into the suite and winced when the floor creaked loudly. He held his breath for a beat, waiting to see if Angel shifted.

No hint of sound came from the bed a few feet away, and he finally let out his breath. He didn't want to wake her. He didn't want to pick up where they'd left off. Didn't know if this time he'd be strong enough to walk away.

Shutting the door quietly behind him, he thought about what she'd said earlier. His wife had done some maturing since they'd parted. He couldn't get over how up-front she'd been. He'd known, hadn't he? When she'd shown up at his suite back in Boston, looking so utterly seductive, he'd harbored no illusions about what her true intent was.

Angeline Scott apparently missed the kind of rough-house, tumbledown lovemaking they'd once shared. Now that was all she wanted from him. She wasn't even shy about admitting it.

So very tempting. What kind of man would that make him if he took her up on it? Knowing that any kind of reconciliation was out of the question. Not if there was any chance of Richard Scott taking his daughter back into the fold.

A chilling thought raced into his brain. What if she didn't miss such physical enjoyment at all? All this time they'd been apart, maybe she had found such release regularly elsewhere. With other men?

He squeezed his eyes shut. It was no business of his. It hadn't been for three years. But the thought came close to physical pain. It took all he had to try to force it out of his mind.

His gaze focused on the outline of her leg. Long, shapely, the white sheet draped seductively around it. He imagined going up to her. Pulling the sheet up and running his hands over the smooth skin, up her leg. Higher.

He thought about the sensuous heat in her eyes as she woke and saw him. He thought about settling over her, feeling her arms go around him, touching his bare back.

Damn. R.J. moved back to lean against the door, and this time the creak was louder.

It would be so easy to go to her. He wanted to so badly. But he wouldn't. Maybe she could be casual about resuming a physical relationship, but there was no way he could be. Not that he hadn't had casual flings himself. He just couldn't with her. Never with her.

He started to settle himself on the floor. No need to bother with a comforter or any padding, he figured. He wasn't going to get any sleep anyway.

CHAPTER EIGHT

ANGELINE STEPPED OUTSIDE into the gentle, warm air of the veranda where Mila, Tavov and R.J. were already seated around the table. A soft morning breeze caressed her bare arms and legs and ruffled the sundress she was wearing. In the distance, she could hear the gentle waves of the sea. Bright sunshine accented the brilliant green of the lush plants surrounding them.

"I hope I haven't kept you waiting," she said, addressing all three at the table. She picked up her dining napkin and sat down, trying to ignore the fluttering in her stomach caused by R.J.'s stare. Dear God, the man only had to look at her and her stomach did jumping jacks.

She'd woken in the middle of the night to find him sleeping on the floor. It had taken all she had not to pull him into bed with her. This morning he had showered silently and beat her downstairs.

"Not at all," Mila answered her. "We've just been discussing the upcoming wedding."

Tavov leaned over and patted his wife's hand. "Mila's very excited. Let me tell you a wedding around these parts is a grand affair."

"Yes indeed." His wife nodded. "There'll be beautiful music, of course a ton of food. The whole village is set to attend. Everyone is just so excited."

Angeline picked up a pastry from the large tray in the center of the table, a filo dough pocket stuffed with various cheeses. Steam rose from the hot center as she broke it open.

Taking a bite, she felt a pang of envy for the bride. How lucky to be looking forward to the rest of your life with the man you loved. She looked over at R.J. and found him staring at her. For a moment she could do nothing but hold his gaze. She had so anticipated their own marriage. By no means was it a grand affair. Just two people so in love they couldn't wait to take on life together.

Mila's voice broke through her thoughts. "I really think you'll enjoy the celebration, Angel. We're going to have folk dancers dressed in traditional costume. They're the best in the area. And you and I will be able to help with the henna ceremony before the reception."

"The henna ceremony?" Angeline asked, intrigued.

"Yes, it's tradition. A craftswoman from the village will brand the young bride's hands with decorative patterns using dark red henna. It's absolutely beautiful. Such a shame it fades in a few weeks.

"The women will do that while the men tease the groom about the chains of married life." She smiled at Tavov. "All the while, they'll be relentlessly filling his glass with ouzo."

R.J. shifted again, and Angel stole a glance at him. He seemed bothered.

"Sounds like a real fete," R.J. declared then, before turning back to Tavov. "I think I'll take you up on the tour of the grounds you offered earlier. If now is a good time."

Angel felt an urge to throw the pastry at him. He was clearly trying to get away. From her.

Tavov nodded. "Yes, yes of course. Whenever you're ready."

"I'm ready right now," he said as he finished off the rest of his breakfast.

The two men stood and made their way toward the orchards. Angeline watched R.J.'s retreating back and then turned to see Mila smiling at her.

"I can tell by the way you're looking at your husband, as if you'd like to chase after him, that this trip is just what the two of you needed. I knew I was right about that. You love him very much, don't you?"

Angeline tried not to gasp out loud. She could only nod. Adoration was definitely not the reason she wanted to chase after R.J. right now.

"It's obvious you and R.J. are committed to each other," Mila continued, oblivious to Angel's true mood. "After all, every marriage has its difficult moments. I think you're the perfect example for the young bride and groom. They're really looking forward to meeting you."

The grin faded quickly. The perfect couple? They weren't even a real couple.

"Um—thank you," was all she could mutter.

Mila suddenly smiled wider. "You know, I have the perfect idea."

Oh, no. Another one of Mila's great ideas. Angel knew she was going to regret what was coming next. "What's that?"

"You and R.J. can offer the young couple a public toast after the nuptials. You know, along with their family and friends."

"Us?"

"Yes of course. Some words of wisdom from a seasoned marriage to one about to bloom."

Angel swallowed. Such a toast would be the most hypocritical thing she'd ever done. There had to be a way to get out of it. But she couldn't see one.

"I—uh— But there must be other people more connected to the couple who would like to do the honors." She knew it was a weak argument.

"Nonsense. It's a rare treat to have newfound friends from so far away attend such a joyous occasion. Besides, what better than to have the lucky tidings of our guests from America to bestow the same good fortune you yourself have enjoyed."

Angel wondered how often in the span of a few days she could be made to feel so horrible. She had no choice but to accept Mila's request. What possible reason could she give to refuse?

"We'd love to do it," she answered. R.J. was going to want to throttle her when he found out.

"That settles it, then," Mila said, rising. "Now, why don't you come with me while I go talk to the chef?"

"Actually, Mila, I was hoping I might be able to walk along the grounds a little. The plants are so lovely to look at."

"Yes, they are, indeed. Even after all these years, every time I look out there, it still takes my breath away." Her eyes grew distant before she sharply turned back to her. "Why don't you wait a few minutes and that way I can accompany you?"

Angel shook her head. "No need to entertain me, Mila. I know you must be terribly busy. I'll enjoy the solitude anyway."

"All right, then. I shall find you for lunch or even run into you sooner perhaps."

Mila nodded and turned to leave, her full-length skirt swirling around her ankles.

"Um, Mila?" Angel stood.

"Yes, dear?"

"Speaking of the plants, would it be terribly harmful to unearth one of them? Perhaps one of the smaller ones?" she asked.

"Certainly."

"Thank you. The scent is just so soothing. I was thinking how nice it would be to have it sit in a vase in our suite while we are here."

"That smell is like no other in the world," Mila agreed. "There are some younger, smaller plants on the southwest corner. You can unearth one of those. I'll go find a vase for you."

"Thank you," Angel replied. Heaven knew she

could use all the soothing and calming of her nerves that she could get whenever she and R.J. were alone in that room together.

"Mila told me I could find you here."

Angel looked up from her crouched position on the ground. R.J. stood above her, his shoulders silhouetted against the bright rays of the sun. Shadow completely darkened his face. He looked like a mythical Greek god, come down from the heavens.

She brushed the dirt off her hands. "Yes, well. Here I am."

"Nice hat," he said with a smirk.

Angeline blew on the netting of the large safari hat Mila had lent her. "Yes, well it keeps the bugs off my face."

He crouched down beside her. "What's that smell?"

She deliberately misread his question. "The plants. They're very floral."

"I don't mean that. What's that awful, antiseptic-like smell?"

"It must be the dirt. It's somewhat damp."

He leaned closer to her and took a sniff. "Darling, I think it's you. New perfume?"

Angel turned and gave him her most vile look. "I'm wearing bug spray, all right? A really strong bug spray. Mila gave it to me."

"It is indeed strong." He didn't even try to hide his smirk. "What are you doing out here anyway?"

She resumed her digging. "I'm removing one of these plants."

"Any particular reason?"

"I just wanted one, that's all." She didn't need to see his face to feel his smirk.

"What for?"

"Just because they're nice. I thought it might brighten up our suite. Don't you think?"

She started digging at the dirt furiously now. The plant root didn't seem to want to budge.

R.J. shrugged, then crouched down beside her. "Well, the plant doesn't seem to want to cooperate in your efforts to dislodge it."

She rubbed her nose with the back of her hand through the netting. Sweat and dirt were starting to cling to her skin. "Nonsense, I've almost got it loosened." Of course, he was right. The plant was barely budging, despite all her efforts.

"If you say so." He absently rubbed a thumb on

her nose through the netting, removing a smudge she must have put there.

Truth was, she was ready to give up just before R.J. had appeared. She'd been in her crouched position for who knew how long, and her knees were starting to ache.

He sighed and settled himself next to her on the ground. "Here, let me help."

"I can do it." She pushed his hand away, suddenly annoyed, though she'd be hard-pressed to say why. Probably from the effort of trying to ignore his closeness and the damp heat around them.

"You said you'd been trying for a while. Just let me help."

She didn't want his help. Didn't need him so close to her, rubbing his arm against her leg. She just wanted to dislodge one little plant. She yanked harder than she should have and ended up falling back on her bottom.

R.J. shook his head. "Why are you so damn stubborn?"

"I am not the one who's stubborn."

"Oh, no? You're sitting in the hot sweltering sun. You have dirt all over you, including on your face." He leaned over and wiped another smudge off her cheek. "But you refuse to let me help. Face it, Angel, you're stubborn. Always have been."

"Fine." She stood with a grunt, unable to bear his closeness any longer. "Go ahead, remove it."

He took another deep breath and got to work on the plant.

"The excitement certainly seems to be buzzing around the estate," she ventured by way of an attempt at conversation. She still had to somehow tell him about this toast she'd just agreed they'd give.

He gave her a brief glance over his shoulder. "You're talking about the wedding."

She dropped to her knees again next to him. "The anticipation about it is almost palpable in the air."

His shoulders lifted in the briefest of a shrug. "Well, I, for one, think it's a bit much."

"Like how?"

"Like do they really need to have over two hundred guests? What's wrong with a small, quaint wedding with close family and friends?"

"How can you say that? Mila and Tavov both said the whole village has been talking about it for months, since the happy couple got engaged, in fact."

He rubbed his eyes wearily. "That's right. I'm sure it will be a loud, crowded, boisterous affair resulting in mass quantities of aching heads the next morning." He stopped tugging on the plant and looked up at the sky. "Exactly the kind of events I usually stay away from. You wouldn't understand."

She wanted to shake him.

"You're right. I don't understand," she said with as much indignation as she could muster. "I think you sound downright heartless." All right, so that was below the belt. But she didn't know what else to say in the face of his negativity.

He suddenly let go of his hold on the plant and braced his forearms on his knees. "What is the big deal about a large wedding? All that matters is that they both say 'I do' and move on. Doesn't it?"

She gaped at him. Move on? This was the most momentous day of these two people's lives so far. R.J. was making it sound like a dental appointment.

"That's one view. A completely boorish, insensitive one," she said.

"Well, it's the one I subscribe to." He turned his attention back to the plant.

"I can't believe you're being so detached about

a young couple's declaration of love and commitment."

"I'm just being practical."

"Well, I think you're being narrow-minded and stiff." She tried to sound as bothered as she was.

"And I think all of you are being fanciful and getting overworked about a simple wedding." He wiped at the sweat on his brow with his forearm. The disdain in his voice had her heart thumping.

She shook her head, flabbergasted at his apathy. "How can you be so negative about this? What kind of toast would you be able to give with an attitude like that?"

He looked up at her. "Huh? What toast?"

Uh-oh. She hadn't meant to spring it on him that way. "Mila wants us to offer the couple a public toast after the nuptials. You know, the old toasting the new."

He looked at her like she'd grown another head. "She wants us to do what?"

"I know what you're going to say and don't bother. I had no choice but to agree to it."

"How the hell are we going to pull that off? Without laughing out loud?"

"I guess we'll just have to demonstrate extraordinary restraint."

The hurt must have sounded in her voice. He let out a breath and rubbed some dirt off his hands. "Sorry. But you gotta admit we have no business toasting such an occasion. I especially don't."

"Why?"

He let out a laugh. "Let's just say my own parents' marriage was an utter insult to the institution. Not to mention our own little effort at holy matrimony."

"You don't really talk much about your parents."

His lips tightened into a firm line. "No, I don't."

And he clearly wasn't going to start now. She hesitated, faltering slightly at the vehemence in his voice.

"Those are not reasons to shun weddings and marriages in general. Haven't you ever had any fun at a wedding ceremony?"

"No." He looked away suddenly. "What about the fiasco your friend Joanne's wedding turned out to be for you? Because of me."

"Joanne had a very pleasant wedding. I had a great time with you."

"Yeah? And it didn't bother you? Not even a little bit?"

"What?"

"Angel, don't play coy. You know exactly what I'm talking about."

"The fact that I was dropped as a bridesmaid? R.J., I was never bothered by that. She just changed her mind about the size of the wedding party. There's nothing wrong with that."

"Is that what you told yourself?"

"What?"

"Come on Angel, she changed her mind about you as a bridesmaid right around the time you married me. You're trying to tell me there's no connection?"

"Of course not. Unexpected glitches come up when planning such events. I understood that. Adjusting a wedding party is not that uncommon."

"Joanne's sudden decision was just a bit too convenient."

"That's just ridiculous." She'd had no idea back then that he'd felt this way. He'd apparently hid so much from her.

"Is that what you really think?" he asked. "Or are you just being blind to your friend's snobbery? You can't tell me you weren't even the slightest bit resentful of me. After all, it was just one more nudge away from your rightful life."

Angel felt her confusion and hurt rapidly convert to anger. "You really think that? That something so silly as a place on someone's wedding party would affect the way I feel about you?"

"It was just more icing on the cake, wasn't it? First your father cuts you off. Then, I can't afford to give you a real wedding. You have to settle for a silly nonevent in a dingy chapel on Roxbury Street. Then you're shunned at one of your best friend's wedding."

She felt the foolish tears and prayed they wouldn't fall. Tears of pain, tears of anger. How shallow did he think she was?

"That 'silly ceremony' was one of the happiest moments of my life, R.J. I'm sorry you couldn't see that."

The look he gave her was one of sheer utter surprise. "Did you think I was faking how happy I was?" she demanded.

"Angel, you had a tendency to tell me what I wanted to hear."

"All I've ever told you is the truth."

He stood up in frustration, his disbelief clear in his stance. "You were happy about turning your wedding day into a fifteen-minute field trip? You were happy about having it rubbed in your face by your best friends that you'd obviously wasted your life and married someone so beneath you?"

She couldn't respond, outraged that he could think so low of her.

"You're telling me none of that mattered to you?" he demanded. "How about how you suddenly lost touch with them all after we were married. All but Shanna."

"We were all busy. Starting new careers. Joanne became pregnant. None of it was intentional."

"That's the reason you stopped associating with your lifelong friends? Busy lives? Not because you'd married someone who would never really fit in at the yacht club events? Someone who'd never swung a golf club, sailed a boat? You're saying none of that had anything to do with how you and your friends suddenly grew apart."

She stepped closer and met him eye to eye. "I'm saying none of that mattered. All that ever mattered to me was being with you." She accentuated every word, daring him to challenge them.

His lips formed a curve that wasn't a smile. "That's what you tried to tell yourself, wasn't it?"

"It's what I believed." She knew she was about to go out on a limb. "It's what I still believe."

He touched her then. The gentlest brush of fingertips across her chin. "My sweet Angel," he whispered. "What I would have given to have that be enough."

She grabbed his wrist, holding it next to her face. "It could have been. It *should* have been." Dear God, why didn't he see?

"R.J., you meant so much more than silly society weddings. You meant more than anything. We did. The two of us."

His noncommittal silence infuriated her. He honestly discounted her loyalty that much. To think that things as trivial as an informal wedding and the shunning from her so-called friends would have made her resent him.

"Why can't you believe that?" She whispered the question, yearning to understand.

His eyes searched her face, but he didn't answer. Finally, he sighed and leaned back over the plant. "If you grab the bottom, I'll yank from the top. It should be enough to pull it out."

That was it. The look in his eyes told her he wasn't going to let her in any further. How could he have hidden such feelings from her? Dear God, she'd been walking through her marriage blind. She'd have done so much differently if he'd only been honest with her. It might have made a difference.

It might have saved her marriage.

She silently lowered herself back over the plant and did as he instructed. Unable to look at him, she gave the plant a forceful yank full of all the frustration and fury she was feeling. This time, the plant slid easily out, finally defeated.

CHAPTER NINE

"THEY'RE AGONIZING."

"I beg your pardon?" R.J. stood up from the table as soon as Mila entered the sitting room.

"She means the tea leaves." Angel was a step behind her. She'd changed into a light black cashmere sweater and a long silk wraparound skirt that hugged her hips provocatively. He tried not to let his eyes run down the length of her legs.

"That's right." Mila smiled at him. "You were staring into the press pot. I thought you might have been watching the tea transform as it brewed. The tea leaves change shape as the water saturates them. It's called the agonizing of the leaves."

Agonizing. He could relate. Angel gave him a knowing look and quirked an eyebrow.

R.J. pulled out the chair Mila was headed for and then waited for her to sit down. He moved toward Angel's chair, but the look she gave him was more effective than a slap on the hand. Their conversation earlier in the field hadn't been forgotten.

"So what have you two been up to all day?" Mila asked.

"Nothing exciting," he answered and thought about how incredibly wrong that statement was.

Excitement and adrenaline were still running through his blood. Her words had replayed in his mind, words that were too tempting. Too dangerous. Words that weren't reality. She might be able to fool herself. But there was no fooling him. It *hadn't* been enough that they'd cared for each other.

They were two breeds that didn't mix. He'd made his peace with that. How dare she try to make him question that now? She was playing with fire, tampering with conclusions made long ago. And now she sat there, looking as innocent as a missionary.

"Did Angeline tell you you're to speak at the wedding?" Mila clapped her hands together. "I've talked to the couple about it, and they're terribly excited."

Angel dropped her spoon with a clang, and he felt some of his anger ebbing. He'd almost forgotten all this was putting a lot of strain on her, too. He suddenly felt like a heel for the way he'd been behaving. Hell, he had to admit it was more than part self-defense. She just had to understand that they couldn't rehash the past anymore. Things could not go any further between them. He had to spend nights alone with her, for God's sake.

"I mentioned it to him earlier," Angel directed at Mila. "He was terribly happy about it." She glared at him.

Angel's tone most definitely did not match her words. Mila lifted curious eyes at the two of them, then resumed sipping her tea.

R.J. cleared his throat. "I'm just not one for public speaking, that's all. It sort of makes me nervous," he embellished.

Angel let out an unladylike snort from across the room. "That's really amazing coming from a high-level, respected CEO."

"Yes, well, it's completely different."

Angel set her cup down. "I find it fascinating, Mila, that a man who can be so successful within the cutthroat business of corporate security can be so deathly afraid of certain things."

"For God's sake." R.J. stood up. He'd have to be a fool not to understand her double meaning.

"Is there a problem?" Mila lifted an eyebrow.

No problem at all. I just don't know whether to shake my ex-wife silly or carry her upstairs.

"None whatsoever," Angel said drily.

"Are you certain, dear?" Mila asked.

"Absolutely. Why do you ask?" Angel's voice dripped with honey. The eyes boring into him told another story, however.

"Is that some kind of new American trend, then?"

R.J. looked down at the clear glass cup Angel was holding and knew immediately what Mila was referring to. He bit back a smile. Angel blinked.

"Is what?" Angel asked.

Mila leaned closer. "I'm wondering why you put both milk and lemon into your tea. Is it a new American thing to drink it curdled like that?"

Angel glanced down into her cup and wrinkled her nose. She recovered quickly. "Not yet it isn't. But who better than me to start one?"

She smiled so wide, R.J. figured it must have hurt her jaw.

Mila wasn't buying it. She kept looking back from Angel's smiling face to R.J. He just shrugged.

"I see," Mila finally said. "I think I'll go have my tea downstairs on the veranda."

"Wait." Angel stood. "I'll join you."

Mila lifted her hand. "No, dear, I don't think

you should." With that she turned and walked out of the room.

"I think that was a subtle hint that she thinks we need to talk." R.J. walked over to the table.

"Yes, well, unfortunately Mila doesn't know any better, does she?"

"On the contrary. I think she's a very wise woman."

Angel sat back down with such a thud he felt himself move to catch her in case she actually missed the chair.

She started to chew her lip. The small action made her lips look so damn kissable.

"R.J., we're doing it again."

He had to refocus. "Doing what?"

"We're messing up."

"How so?"

"Mila is obviously aware there's something not right between us. Tavov is probably suspicious also."

He walked to her and lifted her slowly by the elbow. "Come on."

"Where are we going?"

"We shouldn't be talking about this here."

He guided her toward the balcony adjoining the sitting room. It overlooked the side of the house.

Across them over the horizon, the sun was making a slow dip into the water. Angel moved over and leaned her elbows on the edge of the railing.

God he wanted to go to her. He wanted to pull her toward him, to tilt her head back and drink his fill of her. Their exchange in the fields earlier once again repeated in his mind. The desperate look in her eyes when she'd told him he'd been the only thing that mattered. For one split second there he had believed it. Had wanted so desperately to believe it. It had taken everything he had not to pull her into his arms. To hell with her father's cruel demands. But he couldn't.

So he was acting distant instead.

He felt a sudden pang of guilt. For his behavior, he told himself. Not for his reasons. He had to stay strong and reject his attraction. His strength and his resolve had served him well in adulthood. He was a far cry now from the scared, mousy little boy hiding from his violent father. He needed to pull on all the strength he could muster to do the right thing here.

Of course, Angel didn't know any of that, and it hardly mattered now. She deserved a chance to fully move on, to find someone more suitable so that she could reclaim her rightful position as the sole Scott heir.

On that reminder, he forced himself to remain where he was. He watched as a group of men on the grounds below them started setting up the party-style tents. Others were stringing streamers on the plants and trees along the perimeter.

"Look, we knew things would be a little awkward." He tried not to laugh at the understatement. "But we have to be more careful, judging from Mila's reaction in there just now."

"You're right. And she told me after breakfast that it appeared we were making amends to each other."

"Right, so no more repeats of what just happened in there. Agreed?"

"Agreed. We'll have to act very different," she said without looking up, a slight hesitation in her voice.

He was doubtful, too. Playacting as the loving couple was easier said than done lately. But how the hell was he supposed to convincingly act like the man who still made love to her at night? When all he could focus on was the desperate need to do so and the clear knowledge that it would be wrong.

"Our actions as of late have been less than convincing, but we can work on fixing that," he repeated with more conviction than he felt.

"Certainly." She blew a bang off her forehead. "How?"

How the hell did he know? "Uh—I should probably hold your hand more often."

"I suppose that would be good."

"And I should probably put my arm around you more often."

She nodded emphatically. "Right. And I should pretend to enjoy it."

He snapped his head to look at her. Fury and disappointment rocketed through him until he noticed the small lift at the corner of her mouth. She actually had the nerve to tease him at a time like this.

"See if you can manage to do that," he said drily. "That should allay some of their suspicions."

"And definitely no more arguments," she said, much more serious.

She stared at him. "I just have one question."

Oh, no. "What's that?" he asked, though he really doubted he wanted to answer.

"You're usually Mr. Logical, always focused on the facts. You usually immediately home in on the most reasonable scenario. Why is it that you only appear irrational when it involves me?"

The question caught him off guard. Why exactly did he get so scattered when it came to her? Why did he still feel any sense of responsibility toward his estranged wife?

He turned away from her to walk to the other side of the balcony. "Very good question, Princess. Trust me, my life would be so much easier if I had an answer."

Before she could ask him to expand on that surprising comment, R.J. suddenly stopped in his tracks and turned to her.

"Looks like we have a chance to do some damage control," he whispered.

Damage control? What in the world was he talking about?

Sheer shock replaced her confusion as he gently lifted her chin. The breath caught in her throat, and she was afraid to look up at him, afraid of the sudden change in the conversation.

And then he was kissing her.

Dizziness assaulted her, and he must have noticed. He lowered his hands on her arms and held her closer. The sweet contact with his lips never wavered.

She didn't know why he was suddenly doing this, didn't care. All that mattered now was that he not stop.

She noticed movement in the corner of her eye. It hit her then. Tavov had stepped onto the balcony; he was watching them. R.J. was putting on a show. He was kissing her only for Tavov's benefit.

The hurt opened fire on her heart. All of a sudden it was too much: their arguments, his demands, the tension. And the taste of him, his heat up against her.

Something snapped. She pulled her arms out of his grasp and lifted them around his neck. His sharp intake of breath didn't even make her hesitate. She stepped closer to him, feeling the rock of muscle that lined his frame.

"Oh, we need to be so much more convincing than that…" she spoke low into his ear. "A real wife," she continued, "would be much closer to her husband as he kissed her."

"Angel—" His cautionary warning died on his lips when she rubbed against him.

His arms went slack, then came around her again, tighter this time. A small voice whispered in the back of her brain. She knew she shouldn't be doing this. She shouldn't be baiting him this way.

But somehow her mouth and body wouldn't obey the logic.

"And she'd do a lot more of this."

She boldly touched her tongue to his lips to demonstrate. One of them moaned, she couldn't tell who. Maybe they'd done it in unison. His mouth pressed against hers fiercely, punishing. But the bruising kiss was more than welcome. She needed to see him moved, needed to know that at least some small spark of affectionate passion remained between them. Needed to have him touch her for her, not for the benefit of an audience.

A movement to her left told her Tavov was leaving. R.J.'s quick glance said he'd noticed it, too.

But their kiss didn't stop. His palm splayed at the small of her back, and he hauled her through the miniscule breath of space between them. Waves of pleasure rocked through her at the contact. She became more adventurous and trailed the tip of her tongue along his lips. Finally, he opened his mouth and forcefully took her in. She thought the taste of him would drive her wild. And she wanted it to, wanted to push herself to the edge of sanity and bring him there with her.

This was what her dreams had been about. This intensity she'd never forgotten. She savored the taste of him on her tongue, the feel of him against her body. She was shaking from the inside out. He wanted her. His kiss told her he always had.

He yanked her away suddenly. "What the hell?" he bit out, fury vibrating through his whole body.

It had backfired. She'd tried to elicit some response from him and instead she was the one quaking with desire. He grabbed her by the elbow and led her away from the balcony doors. All traces of gentleness were gone as he pushed her up against the wall.

What a mistake. He'd never been a man to be pushed. Somehow, she made herself meet his gaze.

"Don't play games with me, Angel."

She tried to move away, and he slapped both his palms against the wall on each side of her face. She flinched as he leaned closer, his breath hot up against her skin.

"I already told you not to push for something you're not sure you're ready to give."

She'd hurt him. R.J. attacked only when he was wounded.

Briskly, he took her by the arm and pulled her into the suite, shutting the balcony door behind them.

She cleared her throat. "I—I'm sorry. I know you don't want me to—"

His eyes narrowed, and he cut her off. "It's not about what I want." He cursed under his breath. "The whole problem is how badly I want you still." He rammed a hand through his hair. "But this can't happen between us."

Angel wanted to crawl into a hole in the ground. How many times could she throw herself at this man only to be turned down?

She had to ask the question that had been plaguing her. Couldn't avoid it any longer. "Is there someone else?"

He hesitated a brief moment, as if weighing his response. Finally, he rubbed a palm down his face. "No, there's no one else."

She couldn't help the surge of relief that shot through her. But R.J. still looked downright anguished. "Then what is it? I know there are things you're keeping from me. Things you've never let me in on. I wish you'd just trust me enough to do so now."

He studied her face. "I was trying so hard not to rehash the past on this trip."

"But it keeps coming up, doesn't it? I get it, you're still angry."

"Angry?"

"Yes. That I didn't come with you when you asked. I understand that." She took a deep breath. "I thought you'd come back."

"Oh, Angel. Sweetheart."

"The truth is, I didn't come with you because I thought you'd be back for me. I was so wrong."

He studied her face. "Maybe you're right. Perhaps it is time to come clean about some things."

"Please."

"Right before I got the job offer in Silicon Valley, your father paid me a visit."

Angeline's heart stopped for an instant, then started beating double time. This wasn't going to be something she wanted to hear. "What did my father have to say?"

"He had an offer for me."

"I don't understand." But as she said the words, the realization dawned on her. The offer was a bribe.

"He said he'd make it worth my while to take the job in California. He wanted to pay me to leave. To leave you."

Suddenly, all the pieces fell into place. R.J.'s admission answered so many questions, solved so many unanswered little mysteries: R.J.'s sudden interest in moving far away. For a job he'd barely been interested in when he'd first been offered it.

"I see," she said, trying to process it all. "That explains a lot."

"I didn't want to tell you."

"I wish you had. I could have told you right away that I don't blame you. I'm glad it worked out so well for you."

He blinked. "What are you saying?"

She swallowed past the sickening wave of nausea that had suddenly gripped her. "I'm saying it's okay. I mean, look at all you've accomplished with it."

"Wait. You think I took it. You think I took his money."

That's clearly what he was telling her, was it not? "Isn't that why you left?"

"Is that who you think I am?"

"You mean…you didn't?"

"Of course I didn't" He'd raised his voice. His eyes grew a deeper, darker shade.

He was the one getting angry? "Is that supposed to make me feel better? You didn't take my father's money, but you left anyway. Without telling me anything about what was happening."

"I knew things would never work out. Not with your father's ever-present shadow looming over us. I figured we would either take the leap and both leave, or I'd give you a chance to reunite with the only family you have. I left it in your hands."

"Unbeknownst to me." And *he* was her family by then. He was her husband.

"Your father was willing to pay me a large sum of money to stay away from you. That's the kind of man he thinks I am." He exhaled a heavy breath. "And you seem to think I'm the kind of man who could take him up on it."

She stepped right up to him, jabbed a finger at his chest. So hard her knuckle hurt. "You don't get to play the wounded party here. By keeping me in the dark about this, you made a major decision for both of us."

"Would it have made a difference in the end?

If you'd known?" He grabbed the offending hand and held it in his own. "I couldn't stay there after that."

"You should have come to me. I could have explained it."

"Explained what?"

"That my father pays for everything. It's how he gets his way," she bit out. "But you made it so easy for him. You gave him exactly what he wanted, and he didn't have to pay a dime."

Angeline stood and waited as a breath of a wave slapped around her toes, the water refreshingly cool.

The sea air massaged her face. The effect should have been peaceful, but her heart was still racing, pounding against her chest. She'd abruptly left R.J. alone on the balcony in a desperate attempt to get away. Somehow, some way, she had to get her mind around what he'd just told her.

The damning secret he'd kept from her for three long years.

She heard soft footsteps behind her and realized her respite would be short-lived, however. It appeared R.J. had followed her.

"I need to talk to you," he quietly said behind her. His voice was tight. He drew a breath. "I'm sorry."

"Are you apologizing for what just happened, or what you've been keeping from me all this time?"

He blew out a breath. "Either. Both."

She bit down on the scathing response that came to her lips. What good would that do? What's done was done. "Apology accepted."

"That's it?"

"What else?"

"You have to understand something, Angel. I'm not sure I'd do anything differently if given the same reality today. I did what I thought was best."

Dear heavens. He honestly believed that. "Then there really is nothing else to say, is there?"

She plastered an insincere smile on her face. "Hey, listen. It's okay. Right now, we're business partners, right? Not your everyday garden-variety type but business partners just the same. Let's just focus on that for the time being." She herself had to, or she might just lose her mind on this trip.

It was hard to read his expression.

He nodded once. "Right. Partners."

"Partners," she repeated, trying not to choke on the word.

She turned and started walking again, afraid to look into his eyes any longer.

He continued behind her. "Was there something else?" she asked.

This time he smiled. "Yeah, actually."

"What is it?"

"I think we should leave for a while."

She shook her head, confused. "Leave?"

"Yeah, I think we should get away from the orchards. You know, do some sightseeing or something." The smile turned into a boyish grin. Its effect on her felt like a blow in the stomach.

"Sightseeing? Now?"

"What better time?"

"I thought you said this wasn't a pleasure trip. That we had to do what we came here for and leave."

He looked up toward the horizon. "Yeah, I know. But it occurs to me that we could use the distraction. Let's face it, staying here under Mila and Tavov's watchful eye continuously, it's starting to feel like being in a zoo exhibit or something."

"What about Mila and Tavov?"

"I told them we wanted to take in the sights. And that we didn't expect them to chaperone us, that they were doing enough already."

"They bought that?"

"Not really. I had to insinuate that we wanted to have some time to ourselves, without others around."

"You didn't!"

"Don't worry, I was diplomatic about it."

"I'm sure you were. What did you have in mind?"

They continued walking. Angel let the water lap around her ankles and drench the hem of her long skirt.

"You were right about the island," R.J. said. "It is one of the prettiest areas in the world. The city is supposed to be amazing. Restaurants, shops, a bazaar that could compete with the Grand Bazaar in Istanbul. I think we should go explore it all."

Her breath caught. He hadn't forgotten what she'd said on the flight over here. Though she knew better than to think it was more than an apologetic gesture.

"R.J., you don't need to placate me. I'm a big girl." She wiggled her toes in the water.

"That's not what I'm doing. I just think it would be good to get away for a while, and the city is only about an hour away by car. So why not?"

Why not? Because it sounded like a dream to her, like a fantasy she'd not dared to hope for during the last few years. What would she have given to be able to spend the day with R.J. just a few short weeks ago? Now she was being offered the chance to, even if it was just to assuage his guilt. If she was smart she'd turn him down. Heaven knew her heart wasn't ready for such an experience, not after the conversation they'd just had.

Then again, she certainly could use the distraction.

"I think you should tell Tavov and Mila we've changed our minds," she told him.

He lifted his eyebrows. "You don't want to go?"

"I mean that we've changed our minds about going alone."

His expression shifted. "You'd rather not go alone with me." He turned before she could answer. "I'll go tell them you'd like them to come."

She reached out to touch his arm. "No, not them."

"Then who?"

"Reid and Kaya."

Understanding settled over his features. "The bride and groom."

She nodded. "I think they probably could use the chance to get away, too. And they could show us around like true natives. I know you've been there before, but they've got the insider's track."

He studied her. "It means that much to you to spend this time with them?" he asked.

She nodded, hoping he wouldn't guess as to just why. If R.J. got the opportunity to spend just a few hours with the young couple, if he could just witness firsthand how excited they must be about getting married, maybe it might make the whole idea of toasting at the wedding a bit more palatable. Especially after the conversation they'd just had.

He shrugged. "Why not? It might be fun. Though I'm gonna warn you it's been a while since I've been out on any kind of double date."

"It *will* be fun. Just give me a half hour to get ready."

"All right," he agreed. "I'll go see about securing a vehicle."

She turned away to stare at the water before speaking. "I'm glad you were finally straight with me."

He didn't say anything, his only response a soft sigh before walking away.

* * *

R.J. paid the cabbie and turned to join Angeline and the other couple already at the entrance of the expansive shopping bazaar.

He'd learned about the place when he'd been doing research after the meeting in Angel's office back in Boston. It was one of the biggest indoor bazaars in the world.

He wasn't sure why he was doing this, why he'd even brought it up. But the past few days had just been so tense. They definitely needed the time away. He certainly did, anyway. At least they'd be able to relax a little, away from Tavov and Mila's all-too-observant stares.

He looked up to see a wide smile on Angel's face. With a wave of her hand, she gestured him over to where she stood with Reid and Kaya. He knew when he looked at her what his motivation had been; the joy that was in her eyes right now. He'd been able to put it there quite effortlessly years ago. This little jaunt was a small price to pay to see it there again.

Reid and Kaya were smiling, too, their hands clasped. They couldn't have been older than early twenties. Kaya had the same coloring Angel did, her hair slightly less wavy than Angel's unruly curls. Reid was one of the few blond men he'd seen in this part of the world. He had a small frame and was only slightly taller than his average-height fiancée.

R.J. approached the small group. "Is everyone ready?"

Three happy voices answered him in unison.

"Then let's go spend some money," he said as he placed his palm on the small of Angel's back. It occurred to him that such displays were not necessary now that they were away from the orchard, but it was becoming more and more natural to touch her this way.

Chaos descended as soon as they entered the arched doorway. Hundreds of people bustled past them, and the noise of intense bartering filled the air. Even the decorative artwork on the walls and high arched ceiling seemed busy and detailed.

Kaya turned excitedly to Angel. "We have to look at the jewelry first," she urged. "I bet you've never seen so much shiny gold in one place before."

"I was afraid this would happen," Reid said, his voice suffering. "R.J., we'll never get out of here if the ladies start in on the jewelry. Do you know how many gold stores there are in here?"

"The shine in this part of the bazaar alone is giving me a good indication," he answered.

A teenager breezed past them carrying a dangling tray with small glasses of hot tea swinging to and fro. Miraculously, not a drop seemed to spill.

"I think starting with the gold is a terrific idea," Angel said, smiling wide.

"Hold on to your wallet, my good man." Reid winked at him over Kaya's head. "You're about to buy your wife some baubles."

He felt Angel stiffen slightly next to him. It was natural for Reid to assume that R.J. would be the one making the purchases for her. In reality, aside from her wedding ring, he'd never actually bought her any piece of jewelry. He'd never been able to afford anything worthy of her back then, though he'd always known that someday... And he'd been right. He finally could afford such things. Now that it was too late.

"Well, then. Shall we get started?" Angel offered. "Kaya, lead the way." She gestured in front of her.

"Oh, she knows the way all right," Reid teased.

Kaya pulled her hand out of her fiancé's hand long enough to give him a mock slap on the wrist.

"You really don't want to make me too upset with you in here, do you?" She was giving as good as she got.

Reid gave an exaggerated shudder. "Not on your life. Lead the way, my darling." He stepped aside and bowed.

Angel's throaty laugh shook through R.J. The young couple had such an easy manner between them. He couldn't remember sharing that with any woman. Only Angel had come close, and he hadn't really let it happen. He'd never allowed such camaraderie to occur. *He'd* never allowed it. Despite Angel's warmth, despite her sense of humor. He'd never really let his guard down long enough. It was hard not to feel sorry for that now. He took a deep breath. There was no use questioning any of it.

She'd thanked him for being straight with her. Only there was so much more he didn't ever want her to find out.

The three of them followed Kaya as she made a beeline to one of the merchant booths on the other side. The whole window seemed to glisten like one big treasure chest of gold. He turned to catch a glimpse of Angel. In the dark lighting of the hall, bright yellow from the gold reflected in her eyes, accentuating their distinctive hazel color. He tried not to let the sight take his breath away.

The women were immediately approached by two clerks on the other side of the displays. Neither wasted anytime picking out what she wanted to try on. He couldn't believe he was actually enjoying himself. For all practical purposes, he was being made to shop for jewelry. For the life of him, he knew that should bore him to tears. But quite the opposite, he couldn't remember the last time he'd enjoyed himself so much. Tom, his long-time friend and current business partner, would have a field day if he could see him now. Tom would have to see this to believe it.

Close to twenty minutes later, they were finally out of the store. It was hard to tell which woman had done more damage.

"Did you save any money for the ride home?" he teased Angel. The other couple was walking ahead, immersed in their own world.

"This—" Angel lifted the parcel in her hand "—is a wise investment."

He gave her his best smirk. "Is that what you think?"

"I know it for a fact," she said. "This is high-quality fourteen- and twenty-two-karat gold. You can't find it in the States at these prices."

"What I heard," he began, not ready to stop teasing her, "is that everything in this place is marked up a couple hundred percent."

"Oh, please." She gave him a disdainful look. "What kind of businesswoman do you think I am? I know that. I bartered and negotiated my heart out for these deals."

"I noticed the clerk looked a little exhausted by the time he rang you up."

"I think he was glad to get rid of me."

"It was wonderful," Kaya chimed in as they caught up. "I've never seen anyone haggle so hard. These are some of the best prices I've ever paid."

"Must be hard to be married to a woman who drives such a hard bargain," Reid taunted good-naturedly.

"Absolutely," R.J. agreed quickly. "But it also has its advantages."

"Next store, you can help me seal some bargains, then," Reid said as he stopped to assist his fiancée in putting on one of her recent purchases.

"Be glad to," Angel said. "Actually, R.J., they had some great watches and men's rings. I think a lot of them would have appealed to you."

He lifted a curl of hair that had strayed out of her chignon.

"I'm not much for wearing jewelry, but thanks anyway."

Her expression suddenly turned serious. "Is that why you didn't hold on to your wedding ring?" she asked low enough for only him to hear.

That wasn't a question he'd been expecting. He searched for an answer, something that wouldn't tell her too much.

She suddenly raised a hand to her mouth. "I—I'm sorry," she stammered. "I don't know where that came from."

She appeared as shocked by what she'd said as he was.

"It's all right," he said lamely, still unsure how to respond. What was he supposed to say? Tell her truth? That he had held on to it? That he had it on him even now, and every day since it had been given to him? He couldn't do that.

"Come on, you two." Kaya's excited voice interrupted their mutual discomfort. "We haven't even covered a fraction of territory in here yet."

He gently cupped Angel's elbow and guided her forward. Thank the stars for Reid and Kaya.

Asking them to come along had been a good idea after all.

A few stops later, they were at the door of a large rug and afghan store. This time, the men decided to hover outside while the ladies ogled the merchandise.

"We're really glad you're here to share in our wedding," Reid said.

The wedding. Reid and Kaya had talked about it constantly since the four of them had left the orchard. The more time he'd spent with the other couple, the harder it was to remain jaded or cynical about their upcoming nuptials.

Hell, he'd realized two stores ago that was Angel's intent all along. R.J. suspected she'd invited the other couple along for that very reason. She'd known damn well that he'd have second thoughts about raining on their parade in any way once he got to know Reid and Kaya. And damned if Angel hadn't been right. Damned if he hadn't fallen for it.

He peeked inside the store at her. Angel was traipsing barefoot on a thick, ornate rug. The appealing scene made him feel barbaric enough to want to wrap her neatly up in the carpet, throw the bundle over his shoulder and carry her outside. Then he could wrap himself around her and kiss her with all the want and desperation these past few days had evoked.

He tried to curb his frustration by reminding himself it was almost over. Just a few more days. Once they got through the distraction of the wedding, they could get a signed contract for Angel and head back to Massachusetts. After that, he and his ex-wife would finally go their separate ways. For some reason, that thought didn't have the calming effect it should have.

"R.J., did you hear me?" He looked up to find Reid watching him curiously.

R.J. tried to shake out the cobwebs. "I'm sorry, did you say something?"

The other man let out a small laugh. "You seem a little preoccupied."

"Just admiring the vastness of this place," he lied.

Reid looked at him, then shrugged. "I said it looks like the ladies are about done. What do you say we all grab some dinner?"

"That sounds like a great idea. Any longer with the two of them in here and even this place might run out of merchandise."

Angel and Kaya chose that moment to step

outside. "Angeline, I don't know how you do it," Kaya was saying.

She turned to the two men. "Angeline got that man to go down seven hundred dollars on a hand-woven silk rug."

"Don't be too impressed," Angel insisted. "He must have marked it up at least twice that amount when he saw an American approach."

"Still," the other woman insisted, "they're usually much more stubborn than that."

"Well, even watching all this haggling from a safe distance gave Reid and me a huge appetite," R.J. joked. "Are you ladies through tormenting these poor merchants yet?"

Angel laughed. "Just giving them a taste of their own medicine. It's good for them once in a while."

"Well, we men are worn out. What do you say to some dinner?"

She stepped closer to him. "I, for one, would love to have dinner with said men." She turned back to Kaya. "What about you, partner?"

R.J. noticed Reid's arm go affectionately around his fiancée's midriff. The two of them looked so happy, and so right together. The excitement practically shone from both of them. Excitement about their upcoming nuptials no doubt.

Kaya nodded her agreement. "I know exactly where we can go. This place has the tastiest *doner*. It's a Middle Eastern dish. The perfect combination of lamb and beef, seasoned just right. And on Thursdays and Fridays they have an elaborate show. Both male and female belly dancers."

"Sounds like my kind of place," Angel said. R.J. couldn't help but give her a wary look. Why did she want to watch male dancers? The only one he could picture doing an erotic dance was her.

"Be sure to pay close attention to the dancing, Angeline," Kaya said as the four of them walked out of the bazaar and hailed a taxi.

"Why?" Angel asked.

"Because I'm going to show you how to do it at our wedding," Kaya beamed. "I'm going to show you how to belly dance for your husband."

R.J. didn't bother to suppress his groan.

CHAPTER TEN

"COME ON, ANGELINE. Curve your hips a little more," Kaya ordered with a laugh. The young bride was teaching her a basic belly dancing move. At least she was trying to.

The marriage ceremony performed earlier had been breathtakingly touching, even though part of it had been recited in a dialect Angel hadn't understood. But it had sounded sacred and poetic.

Now the reception was fully under way, with loud pounding music, lively dancing and a lot of food and drink.

"Kaya, I would have to be double-jointed to curve it any more than this."

"All right." The other woman laughed. "I suppose that's good enough."

"It will have to be, unless I want to throw my back out."

"Look, there's your husband. We will start now. Remember what I told you." Kaya winked at her.

"Got it." Angeline quickly lifted the veils up

to cover her face. The fluttering in her stomach wasn't nervousness. She was just playing a game.

Still, it was a risky game. She and R.J. had been nothing more than civil toward each other the last couple of days, ever since the evening they'd spent in the city. They behaved like lovers during the day, then he quietly settled himself down on the floor to sleep at night. She'd offered to share the bed, purely platonically. But he'd refused each time. Still, the friendliness was much better than the cold distance he'd insisted when they'd first gotten here. She didn't want to jeopardize that.

But what was the harm in a little flirting? They still had to be convincing for Mila and Tavov, didn't they?

She turned to look for him in the crowd. Her heart fluttered as she laid eyes on him. He was so striking and handsome. He was at least half a head taller than anyone else there. He looked the epitome of dashing. He looked so darn sexy. He looked dangerous, he looked…downright preoccupied.

Her heart did a little flip when she realized he was looking for her.

Finally, their eyes caught. For one small moment, the world between them seemed to shift.

She couldn't turn away from his stare, and the expression on his face held her spellbound. It was broken when he broke eye contact and started making his way toward her.

"What's this?" R.J. reached her just as the last scarf was securely fastened.

"It's the bridal rites."

He lifted one eyebrow, a smile creasing the corners of his mouth.

"The bridal rites, huh?"

"That's right. It's a way to honor the wedding. All the couples are supposed to kiss at the sound of the chime." As soon as the words left her mouth, the ringing of a nearby bell sounded.

"There it is. You're supposed to kiss me now."

"Yeah?" He lifted an eyebrow and rubbed his chin. "How do I know it's really you under there?"

"You'll know as soon as you kiss me," she couldn't help but taunt him.

R.J.'s expression didn't change, but something shifted in his eyes, and the fluttering in her stomach increased.

"In that case…" He slowly removed the scarf.

She knew her breath had just stopped as she watched him lean closer. Some magnetic force lifted her arms to link her fingers behind his head.

Soft at first, gentle and sweet. His mouth slanted over hers comfortably. He paused long enough to give her a smile, then returned. She ventured to touch his lips with her tongue.

Then fire quickly took over. It molded them together, branding them. His hand splayed at the small of her back, and desire rocketed through her whole being.

He was kissing her the way he had during all those heat-filled needful moments years ago. In an instant, she was back to being the young college student who had fallen so deeply in love with him.

Finally, R.J. broke away. It was hard to tell which one of them was breathing faster. The crowd had gone past the ceremony. Everyone but the two of them had resumed celebrating.

Kaya's joyous peal of laughter brought Angel's attention back to the dance floor.

"She's beautiful, isn't she?" Angel asked. "I don't think I've ever seen a more beautiful bride," Angel whispered as she watched the younger woman swirl around the installed wooden dance floor.

R.J. didn't respond right away. She looked up to catch him watching her. Something in his eyes took her breath away.

"I have," he said in a heated whisper.

He reached out to touch her, his fingers stroking her jaw. The noise of the loud reception around them turned to a faint humming in her ears.

"*My* bride," he added, his tone possessing.

His words shattered her emotions. She lifted shaky fingers to his face. "I—I can't help but think how excited I was the day we were married," she confessed. "Every time those two kiss, I remember how in love we were."

"I've never forgotten." He seemed surprised that the words had left his mouth.

His thumb continued to rub her jaw gently. Her eyes loaded heavy with tears. Tears of regret at what they'd once had and lost.

She searched his eyes for answers. "How did it happen, R.J.? How did we let it slip out of our hands?"

"I wish I knew, darling, but I don't."

Did that mean he was as sorry as she was that it had? Or was this just sentimental rambling brought on by memories forced to the surface.

The emotion in his eyes looked genuine, but she wished she knew for sure. One thing she did know, she'd been fooling herself for years. Her feelings for R.J. went way beyond the physical, way beyond mere attraction.

"There you two are."

Angel jumped back as if stung. She'd forgotten where they were. Tavov and Mila we're walking toward them. Mila had the smile of a royal queen on her face.

"It seems this romantic mood has affected everyone," Mila teased.

Angeline dared a look at R.J. He was staring at her. Fire still burned in his eyes, stoking the one burning in her.

"Come, you two." Tavov motioned. "We're going to stop the music long enough for a couple of more toasts, including yours."

She managed to finally tear her gaze away from R.J.'s heated stare. "That, um, sounds lovely."

Mila stepped to her and took her arm into her own. "Come, our guests are all looking forward to hearing from you."

Angeline nodded, and awareness ran down her spine as she walked away with Mila. She knew R.J. was still watching her.

What was she doing? She'd just managed to shatter any peace she may have obtained. Then realization of the truth erupted within her chest.

She was still in love with him. She always had been. All those years of pretending they'd had nothing but chemistry between them had been such a ruse. Her pretense now stared her in the face. Nothing she could say or do from now on would allow her to deny it anymore. She'd loved him since she'd laid eyes on him. Without a doubt, she wanted him. And he wanted her.

Was that enough?

She shook her head briskly as Mila led her away. What a silly question. Of course it was. Her foolish heart would settle for anything he gave her. That's how blindly in love she was. Something had shifted between them tonight. They had both acknowledged their mutual attraction. And that they'd both felt sentimental for all they'd lost. But she was almost certain for him that's all it was.

She harbored no illusions that he felt as strongly for her as she did for him.

In a few short hours they'd be back in the suite alone. Their spoken words of sentiment still between them. The question was, was she ready to do something about it?

Mindlessly, she followed R.J. up the steps to the portable stage. Another man was already at the microphone offering his best wishes.

Angel didn't hear him. How in the world was she supposed to go back to her carefully crafted life after this? The one belief that had helped her move forward was the knowledge that it would take only a matter of time to get over a youthful attraction. Now she would have to acknowledge the pain for what it was—her heart breaking, slowly and irreparably, with each and every day, most likely without end.

"We're being called forward, Angel."

"What?"

"It's our turn to toast the bride and groom. And offer wise words of guidance." He seemed to have a barely veiled grip on his control. Was he as floored as she was? Or was it just all this acting starting to take a toll on him, as well?

Letting him guide her toward the center, she pasted what she hoped was a convincing smile on her face. Suddenly, the true force of what she was about to do hit her. She felt the eyes of hundreds of people, waiting for her to say something. People who had no reason to suspect she was being anything less than sincere.

"Well, Angel?" R.J. prompted.

"Huh?"

"What's your answer?" For some odd reason,

she felt her nervousness go down a notch at the sound of his voice.

"I'm sorry, I didn't hear your question."

"Would you like me to go first?" he asked.

What a godsend. "Y-yes, thank you. I guess I should have been better prepared. It's a little different from a business presentation, isn't it?"

He merely tipped his head in answer.

"I'm sure I'll come up with something concrete by the time you finish." She hoped she would.

"It's okay. I'm not exactly sure what I'm about to say myself."

She watched as he took the microphone from the bride's waiting cousin. The crowd seemed to grow even quieter as R.J. cleared his throat.

"First of all," he began, "I'd like you all to know what a terrific honor this is for both me and my wife." Angel swallowed at the last word.

"We were honored to be invited, and we are even more pleased to be able to personally give our regards to the couple."

The crowd had grown completely silent, hanging on R.J.'s every word.

"I know everyone's got a lot of celebrating to do, so I'll be brief. To our honored couple, I'd just like to say…remember always what has brought you here together to this day. No matter how little, remember every detail that has endeared you to each other."

Angel felt herself chewing her lip. It would be so easy, so terribly tempting to believe his words actually held some meaning for the two of them.

R.J. continued. "Never take for granted the love you have for each other. It is a gift that few people are ever lucky enough to find. It's apparent when looking at the two of you that you have done so. So remember the little treasures, remember the starlit nights, the slow dances when it's just the two of you on the dance floor. Remember how the other person's smile takes your breath away." He stopped to clear his throat, and Angeline felt her eyes sting. What she wouldn't give to have those words come from him directly to her.

But she had to be logical. She had to realize that fate was playing a cruel, harsh joke on her. Forcing her and R.J. to utter words that may have been true years ago but had long ago lost their merit. She blinked the tears out of her eyes as R.J. resumed his speech.

"And finally," he continued, "always remember, nothing matters but the two of you and what you've found in each other." He lifted his glass before completing. "Good luck and best wishes." The crowd stood silent for the briefest of seconds and then roared their applause.

Angel was too stunned to move—let alone speak. She felt R.J.'s hand at her elbow nudging her toward the crowd. He handed her the microphone.

She cleared her throat and winced as the sound tore through the air. "Well, that's going to be quite a tough act to follow.

"Again, we are both so very pleased that you have made us part of such a joyous occasion. My husband pretty much put it best. Fate has brought the two of you together. The love you share for each other has culminated in this very special moment. It stands stronger than time. True love transcends pride, wealth and—" she turned to look fully at R.J. "—background."

At the last word, she had to turn away from him.

"So from this day forward, let your affection for each other be the power that guides you. Let nothing or no one ever tell you it's any less than it is. R.J. and I will always remember how strong your bond is. Good luck and best wishes."

The band struck up behind her as the crowd cheered, but Angeline stood frozen where she was. Adrenaline pumped through her, and it had nothing to do with public speaking.

"Nice words," R.J. whispered in her ear.

"Thanks. For a moment I wasn't quite sure what I was going to say. I'm glad it's over."

He was about to respond when he was interrupted as Tavov clapped a hand on his shoulder.

"R.J., good speech. There's someone here I'd like you to meet."

"Please, go on," she urged before he could refuse. She didn't feel much like celebrating.

He appeared out of nowhere. Angel shook the sleep off and sat up. She could see R.J.'s silhouette through the darkness. He had the advantage. The bed was bathed in moonlight while he stood protected by the black cover of the night.

"R.J.? Are you all right? I've been so worried." She glanced at the mounted clock on the wall. "It's almost dawn.

He didn't answer, didn't move.

She removed the covers and started to get out of bed. "Where have you been? You've been gone for hours." She realized too late her state of disarray. Her pajama top had shifted off her shoulders, exposing most of her neckline and chest. She knew R.J. had noticed.

She drew the covers protectively back around her.

"I was trying to stay away," he whispered. "Away from this room, away from you." She heard him suck in a deep breath. "But I couldn't do it. I'm not strong enough."

His voice sounded off, strange. She could barely make out his shape. Some internal battle he was fighting was evident in his tone. He moved closer, and Angeline felt her heart beating furiously in her chest. It was fear and anticipation all at once. Her hands stilled, fingers wrapped tightly around the blanket.

"I tried so hard not to come back here. Because I knew I wouldn't be able to help myself if I was back in this room with you. But here I am."

She swallowed, willed herself to speak. "Where'd you go?"

"I've been wandering the beach for hours. I think I may have walked to the next city over before turning around."

Angel resisted the urge to stand and hug him; he'd been wandering in the chilly dark night. "We knew this wasn't going to be easy. Pretending to be married, I mean."

He shook his head. "That's been the easy part. Pretending I can resist you is what I can't stand anymore."

She knew it was really him, knew she wasn't dreaming. But the voice she heard now didn't belong to the man she'd known before. This sounded like a man whose last hold on control had just snapped.

"What caused all this?"

He let out a small laugh that sounded wounded and bitter. "Everything. The wedding, how happy Reid and Kaya seem to be starting their lives together. Our toast. Even watching Mila and Tavov, seeing how happy they still seem after all these years." He paused for so long she thought he wasn't going to speak again. But then added, "And watching you. Pretending you're still mine. Trying to ignore the way you affect me."

She bit down on her lip. "And how do I affect you, R.J.?"

"Like no one else ever has. Apparently three years apart hasn't changed it."

Her breath caught at his admission.

"But you have to tell me," he continued. "I'll

walk out of here right now if you want me to. God knows, it's the sane thing to do. But if that's what you want, you'd better tell me now."

She couldn't form a response, couldn't bring herself to speak. It took all she had to resume breathing. Finally, she summoned the ability to utter his name.

"Come here," he bade. The gentlest of demands, as if he'd finally allowed himself to voice a silent wish.

Her limbs wouldn't move. Heavens, she wanted him, wanted to feel him around her, embracing her. Over her. Yet an overwhelming force held her where she was, unable to move past the crossroads she was being offered. If this was the wrong move, she knew without a doubt that this time her heart would never recover.

"I need to be certain, Angel." She heard his scratchy voice through the darkness. "I need to be sure this is what you want. Show me." He paused to take a deep, tortured breath.

Suddenly, without preamble or warning, she felt her own slim grasp on control snap.

Somehow she managed to move, though she wouldn't have thought it was possible. The hardwood floor felt cold on the soles of her feet, but the sensation barely registered. The universe consisted of nothing but the man before her. The man she knew she would always love. True to form, he was making sure it was completely her decision.

Automatically, she placed one languid foot in front of the other. He stepped closer to her, and the moonlight finally illuminated the hard, sharp features of his face. The harsh reality of what she was about to do hit her when she fully saw his face.

And then she could go no farther. Only the length of a small room stood between them. But it may as well have been miles. Nothing and everything held her back. Fear, desire, desperation, doubt. All of it warred within her, freezing her in her spot. Even in his cry for her, she could feel part of him holding back. Perhaps the most important part.

But what was the point in fighting? She couldn't deny she wanted him. Would always want him.

Her need for his touch roared like wildfire in her ears. She reached out her hand, asking silently for reassurance.

R.J. quickly breached the area between them. The contact was sudden, savage. She knew the world had stopped. At least it had for her.

He grabbed her by the waist and pulled her

fiercely up against him. The kiss was clumsy at first. Then sheer familiarity took over. She savored the taste of him.

He thrust forceful fingers through her hair. Several tangled strands caught, causing a flash of pain. It didn't matter. He kissed her deeper, and she couldn't help the groan that escaped her.

Finally, he was here. And he was going to make love to her.

CHAPTER ELEVEN

HE'D LEFT HER. Angeline knew instinctively that R.J. had moved off the bed. The comfortable warmth that had enveloped her till morning, even in sleep, had disappeared. Squinting in the dawn's light, she made out his silhouette on the balcony.

He looked deep in thought.

Don't panic, he's simply processing. No way he's about to break your heart again.

But her mouth had gone dry.

"Watching the sunrise?" she asked with false cheeriness as she stepped outside. The rigid hold of his back stoked her fears.

This was not going to be a fun conversation.

He didn't look at her, just kept staring straight ahead at the water. The rays of the infant sun turned the sky a majestic red along the horizon. R.J. had pulled on only his pajama bottoms, his upper body bare despite the chill. Her gaze fell to his chiseled arms. Arms that had held her into the morning. Surrounded her and loved her.

There was no mistaking the tension in his shoulders.

He didn't look at her when he spoke. "I'm afraid I let all the excitement of last night get to me."

"Is that all that was? The only reason you made love to me was due to the excitement of the wedding?"

"Yes."

She knew better. "I don't believe you. You said a lot of things last night. Things that just don't jell with what you're trying to tell me right now." She stepped closer.

"That was just the heat of the moment, Angel."

Ouch. That dart had hit its mark. But she wasn't going to fall for it. This was nothing more than R.J. trying to battle his demons alone. As usual. "I don't believe that either. Please tell me why you're pulling away."

"This is exactly why I should have stayed away from you last night. We don't need this distraction right now."

"The obvious fact that we still have feelings for each other is a little more than a distraction, R.J. What are we going to do about it?"

"Nothing. We're going to go back to the States and pretend none of this ever happened."

"And move forward with the divorce?"

He tilted his head slightly in agreement. He couldn't mean that. How could he still want the divorce after what had been happening between them on this trip? "We're as different as two people can be, Angel."

She couldn't seem to get through to him. "Why do you still believe that? As far as we've both come?"

"I can say it because it's true. I can declare we're different because while you were out boating with your wealthy friends as a teenager, I was defending myself from my old man. And I usually got a jaw full of loose teeth for it."

Angel felt the breath leave her. "I—I'm sorry. I know you'd had a rough childhood—but you never told me the specifics."

"What was I supposed to tell you? Was I supposed to discuss my life in the projects with my beautiful, privileged Brahmin wife? Was I supposed to tell her how my old man got off on seeing other people suffer, particularly my mother? Was I supposed to explain how I watched her wither from disease and die of cancer in a shelter while he gambled away the little money we had? Money she scraped together by cleaning houses and scrubbing toilets, by the way. In houses owned by people like you."

"I'm so sorry," she repeated, unprepared for the onslaught of emotion pouring from him.

"What do you think about your husband now?" he demanded.

She swallowed the lump that had formed in her throat. "I respect him more than ever."

His eyes narrowed on her. "What?"

"You heard me," she said, firmly. "Look at all you've accomplished despite all that. Look at the life you've built for yourself."

"None of that changes where I came from."

"And what does that mean? Why does it even matter anymore where you came from? You've always been the same strong, bright, talented man you are right now." She'd grown frustrated now. He could be so obstinate. "I see ladies from run-down homes and squalid backgrounds change their lives all the time. It's what the Works program is all about."

"It's not the same thing," he argued.

"Only because what you've done is even more extraordinary." She took a fortifying breath to try to settle her nerves. "No one wants you to forget," she urged. "I certainly don't. You should be so proud of yourself, R.J., for having come as far as you have."

She watched as his hands tightened on the balcony railing. "What about what I did to you?"

Huh? "I don't understand."

He turned to her, his eyes darkened with an emotion she couldn't name. "I cost you everything, Angel. I'm the reason your father won't speak to you. The reason you've lost touch with your friends. I'm the reason you'll be denied your rightful inheritance and your stature as a Scott. You've lost everything because of me."

"My father and I have had a strained relationship since I was a child. It began when my mother left. As for the rest, you can't mean to think any of that matters to me."

"But it should."

She had to laugh at his logic. Until she heard his next words.

"Those are all things that should matter to you, Angel. Because this isn't going to work between us. We don't have a chance."

No, she certainly didn't feel like laughing anymore. Maybe she wouldn't ever again, in fact. "What do you mean?"

"Simple. I'm not husband material. My move to

the West Coast was just a start. I haven't stayed
in one place for more than a couple months since
I left Boston. Don't you see?" He turned from
the railing to fully face her. "I don't want to be
tied down. Not to any one place. Not to any one
person."

CHAPTER TWELVE

WHY THE HELL hadn't he stayed away from her last night? Because he was a selfish bastard who'd ignored everything but his own needs.

R.J. reached down to adjust the shower knob. Turning it, he braced himself for the punishing pulse of hot water.

What a mistake. He'd had to hurt her. She would never understand why they couldn't get back together. Angel could claim all she wanted that her relationship with her father had been strained for years, but the fact was they'd *had* a relationship until he entered the picture.

He couldn't bear the responsibility of being the final knife that ultimately severed their bond, tenuous as it may have been.

Nothing he'd told her had been a lie. It was truth that he was gone for several months at a time. Often not even in the country. What kind of a husband could he be given his lifestyle? Certainly not someone worthy of causing the kind of loss that

Angeline had to endure because she'd married him. The best thing he could do for her would be to sever all contact. And move forward with the divorce once and for all.

At least this fiasco of a trip had opened his eyes to what he needed to do. Best thing now would be to wrap it up.

He had to leave. As soon as he could.

He turned the shower knob even farther, the water almost at scalding now. He would just tell her that a business matter had come up that needed his immediate attention. Hell, that would actually prove the point he'd just made. She couldn't count on him or depend on him to follow through.

And she would see right through it.

No matter. For her own good, he couldn't be around her any longer.

Angeline couldn't seem to make herself move off the balcony. She had no idea how long she'd been standing there listening to the running of R.J.'s shower. She'd barely noticed when the water had shut off and he'd moved about the suite getting dressed.

She couldn't speak to him. She didn't know what to say.

She'd been his wife, but she'd never known about the horrors he'd lived through growing up. He hadn't trusted her enough to share any of it with her. Just like he hadn't trusted her enough to tell her about her father's attempted bribe.

She had to take him at his word now. He just declared to her that he wasn't one to feel close to anybody. He had no interest in being tied down. R.J. had clearly never felt about her the way she had felt toward him.

She certainly wasn't going to beg him to reconsider. He'd done enough by agreeing to this trip.

Shutting her eyes, she inhaled deeply. This wasn't the end of the world. She'd find a way to live her life. She'd throw herself in her responsibilities at TeaLC and with the Works program, and soon, hopefully, this wretched pain in her chest would turn to a dull ache that she might even be able to ignore.

She could do it. She could learn to somehow love him yet live without him.

She finally turned around and stepped back into the gloomy darkness of the suite. Her eyes fell on the unmade bed. Walking over to it, she ran her hands over the tangled sheets. Memories assaulted her, further stretching her already tight emotions. Her gaze shifted to the floor, where the casual white shirt R.J. had been wearing lay crumpled on the floor. Without thinking, she reached for it and put it on. The fabric smelled of him. She rubbed her arms and hugged the material close.

She couldn't bear to take it off. She'd hide it with a spring sweater. She needed to feel near him. And if the best she could settle for was to wear his shirt for the day, then she'd take what she could get.

After all, healing didn't happen overnight, did it?

Angel spent the morning roaming the grounds, trying to clear her scrambled mind. It didn't help. But one thing was certain—she had to tell Mila and Tavov the truth: that TeaLC wasn't going to be run by a family operation after all. It would just be her. They had a right to know. The farce had gone far enough. And she was just tired. Tired of pretending, tired of the half-truths she'd been sprouting to get this deal. Maybe Mila and Tavov had grown to care for her enough that it wouldn't matter and they would hopefully give her the deal anyway. If not, well, she would have to figure out how to grow the business some other way.

As for the prospect she didn't want to think about—if she had to sell, she'd make sure to negotiate the best deal she could for her employees. But she would exhaust every other option first. Every possible loan, every potential investor. None of the choices were ideal. More investors meant more decision-makers who might want to phase out the expensive Works program.

She vowed not to let that happen.

R.J. was already in the suite when she made her way back. There was no missing his closed suitcase in the corner of the room.

"You're back," she announced as she entered the room, careful to keep all emotion out of her voice.

"Just got in."

"Tavov and Mila are expecting us for lunch."

He drew in a breath and looked away. "Actually, I need to talk to you. I'm not going to make it for lunch. Or dinner."

"I don't understand," she lied. She understood all too well, and her heart sank to her stomach.

"I'm leaving."

Her chest felt as if she'd just gone over a steep

drop. "The plan was that we would leave in three days."

"I'm afraid I'm needed back for an emergency a major client is having."

Right.

"I see," was all she could manage.

Don't beg him, whatever you do, don't plead for him to stay.

He'd made his decision very clear. No point in telling him now that she was about to admit to the Bays the entire truth. What did it matter? He wasn't even going to stay.

"But I didn't want you traveling back alone."

A small spark of hope ignited deep within her heart. "I don't understand."

"I've made arrangements to fly Shanna here. She should be arriving tomorrow. The two of you can fly back to Boston when you're ready."

"I guess you've thought of everything."

"We said we'd come together, and we did. Mila and Tavov aren't suspicious. You'll get what you need."

If she was lucky. And even if everything he said proved true, she knew she'd still feel like her world had fallen apart.

CHAPTER THIRTEEN

SHE WAS SUCH a pansy. She couldn't even watch him leave. Angeline stopped in the middle of the rows of tea plants and breathed in the spicy aroma.

He'd be on his way off the plantation now. An overwhelming cloud of sadness shrouded her. Her emotions were all her fault. R.J. had been more than fair with her. He'd gone along with the plan, helped her with the deception, and he'd been honest with her from the beginning. Yep, he'd stuck to his part of the deal perfectly. She'd been the one to let the closeness of it all go to her head. She'd been the one who'd let daydreams cloud her visions.

And now he was leaving. He probably hated himself for letting things go as far as they had. He'd said all along that he wanted nothing to do with her. Pretty soon, the whole business deal would likely go bust, too, as soon as she sat down with Mila and Tavov this afternoon.

She had to tell them.

It was past time to come clean about everything. Past time to let them know that she and R.J. had been pretending all along. Given how much she'd lost, the least she could do was be honest with the people she had grown to care for.

Mila and Tavov had a right to know who exactly they were doing business with. Or not doing business with.

No herbal tea supply, no expansion, no growth in sales.

No R.J.

She closed her eyes against the pain. This time hurt almost more than the first time she'd lost him. Almost.

She'd let him walk out of her life then, too. It had settled nothing. And here she was, years later, experiencing it all over again.

She hugged her arms across her chest, bracing against the tightness in her heart. A small object in the pocket of the shirt she was wearing pressed against her wrist. R.J.'s shirt. She still hadn't taken it off.

Curious, she took off the sweater to look inside the shirt pocket. A shimmer of bright gold reflected out at her. She took the object out.

A thin rope chain with a gold band dangled

from her fingers. Her mind went numb when she realized what it was. R.J.'s wedding band, the original one she'd given him five years ago. The one he'd told her he'd gotten rid of.

He *had* kept his ring.

The implications were almost too much to fathom. He hadn't been able to forget her. Not only had he kept his wedding ring, he still wore it around his neck. All this time, all these years. He'd wanted a token of their love with him always.

Her vision blurred as she stared at the gold. He'd been so good at keeping his feelings from her. Maybe he didn't even want to truly face them himself. It appeared neither one of them was over their breakup.

What was she going to do about it?

Stand by and let the worst loss in her life repeat itself? Without so much as a true answer? Didn't she owe it to herself to at least try to find out exactly what R.J.'s feelings were? Didn't she owe it to both of them? He insisted on being stubborn and distant. But he cared enough to drop everything to participate in a farce of such grand proportions. And he cared enough to want to keep his old wedding ring with him at all times.

She clutched the chain in her palm. Maybe, despite all that, he truly wanted to forget her and go on with his life. Maybe it didn't go any deeper than a genuine affection. But one thing was certain. This time she was going to find out. Her whole future depended on it, and she refused to leave it up to chance or pride. R.J. wasn't the only one intent on not letting history repeat itself.

She owed it to both of them to tell him straight out—ask him not to let her father, or anyone else, come between them this time.

She turned on her heel to find R.J. and get an answer once and for all. She turned to make her way back to the house. It was time to end the doubts. Time to get to the bottom of everything once and for all.

She hadn't taken more than two steps when the putrid smell of smoke hit her nostrils. Then she noticed the flash of deep orange light just a few feet away.

Before the fear even registered, she turned to try to run through the thick and heavy foliage. A fire.

The Mila's Bloom fields were ablaze. And the flames would reach her at any moment.

He had no reason to feel guilty. R.J. grabbed the last of his things from the room he and Angel had shared for the past several days. Zipping up his overnight bag, he paused to look around once more at the room. The same room they had spent days in as man and wife.

The phoniness of it all sent a wave of bitterness through him. He knew Angel would get the deal she had come down here for. He'd played his part well.

Aside from falling for his wife again, that is. There was that one small glitch.

He swore out loud. Whom was he kidding? He'd never fallen *out* of love with her. Still, he could leave now with a clear conscience. The contracts were about to be signed, and Shanna was on her way to escort Angel back.

There was no reason for him to stick around. He'd only hurt her further if he stayed. All he'd ever managed to do was confuse her, and hurt her in the process.

She was a Scott. A true Boston Brahmin. She had certain obligations. People had expectations of her. None of which involved marriage to a hood from the projects of South Boston.

He'd contact Richard Scott as soon as he returned to the States. To let him know he was moving forward with the divorce and that Richard should make plans to contact his estranged daughter. The rift between them had gone on long enough. It was time for Angel to resume her rightful place in the world she'd been born into.

What a mess. He was deeply in love with a woman from one of New England's most prominent dynasties. But he wouldn't allow that love to cost her everything she'd known her whole life.

That's why he had to leave now.

He debated conducting another search for an object that seemed to have disappeared.

You've lost it. It's gone.

If he delayed much longer he'd miss his flight. Besides, maybe it was a telling sign that he'd misplaced his original wedding band. Still, to have lost it after all this time. But he had to let it go. There was no more time left to look for it. He had to let *her* go, too.

He'd already bidden farewell to the Bays and had packed everything else. Angel had disappeared. It was better this way. This time she was the one being logical about things. There was no reason to prolong their leave-taking.

Rubbing a palm down his face, he walked over to the phone. It was time to call for his ride to the airport. He picked up the receiver, then dropped it back into the cradle at the sound of a knock on the door.

Damn. Not right now. He just needed to get out of here. The sooner, the better.

"Yeah?" He knew he sounded curt.

"It's Mila. May I come in?"

What did she want? They'd already said their goodbyes.

"Sure," he answered, despite what he was thinking. "But I'm afraid I don't have much time."

"I see you're packed," Mila said as she breezed into the room.

"Yep. Just about to leave." He threw his toiletries case in the carry-on bag.

"It's too bad you got called back to your office. The four of us could have celebrated signing the contracts tonight." She moved over to the bed and sat down, watching him with probing eyes.

"Angel will have to do enough celebrating for both of us. I've been away long enough," he said, somewhat terse. He didn't want to be rude. He just wanted to get as far away from here as possible.

Mila seemed intent on delaying that.

"I hardly think that's possible," she said. "It's clear from the way she looks at you how much she enjoys your company. She seems to light up when the two of you are together."

Apparently, he and Angel were pretty good actors after all. They had Mila believing wholeheartedly they were a happy young couple still in love. Then again, they weren't acting 100 percent of the time, were they?

"That sounds a little exaggerated," he said and zipped up his garment bag.

"I don't think so. You get a little spark in your eye as well when you look at her, you know."

Man, this was the last thing he needed to be hearing right now. "She is my wife," he managed to say.

"I think it's marvelous."

"What's that?" he asked. Where was all this leading?

"Well, between all of us, we seem to cover the whole range of happy couples."

"Not sure what you mean, Mila."

"Well, there's Reid and Kaya, representing the newest of the group. They've just started the dawn of their life together. You and Angel are in the middle of the spectrum, so to speak." She paused a moment. "How long did you say you've been married?"

There didn't seem to be any way to avoid answering her question. "About six years," he told her. But we've been apart for three, he added silently in his head.

Mila nodded. "Then there's me and Tavov. We're clearly the most seasoned of the group. Do you know we've been married twenty-three years?"

He had to give that the credit it was due. "That's amazing, Mila. And impressive."

She smiled wide. "Yes, and to think no one thought it would last."

His curiosity stirred. "Yeah?"

"Oh, yes. Everyone was convinced we didn't have enough in common. You see, when we met, Tavov had nothing but his dreams. My parents had worked hard all their lives to give me a safe, secure life. They didn't think I should risk my future with someone who had nothing."

R.J. had stopped packing, fully interested in the story now.

Mila continued, a faraway look in her eyes. "But I knew exactly how happy he could make me. I believed in him. We invested every penny of my trust fund toward these orchards. I had every faith that no matter how the investment turned out, Tavov was meant for me. And I was right.

Even if he hadn't discovered and cultivated such a popular product, all I really needed from him was the love he's shown me all these years. Of course, we've had our problems, everyone does."

R.J. was starting to get the distinct feeling there was a message intended for him. But why?

Mila stood up off the bed. "Well, that's enough useless musing from an old woman." She walked over to him and placed a motherly palm on his cheek. "I wish you could stay a little longer."

She moved to the door and left before he could respond.

His thoughts shifted to Angel. He had to see her once more. He honestly didn't know if it had anything to do with what Mila just said. But he couldn't leave just yet, not with things as they were.

Hell, he just had to look into her eyes one more time. All logic aside.

He walked over to the balcony to see if he could spot her on the grounds. A small glow coming from the fields caught his eye.

He squinted in the light to make out exactly what it was. Clarity and horror struck at once. There was no way to jump down the three stories. He turned and started running downstairs.

God, don't let her be in the tea fields.

"Tavov," he bellowed, not pausing to see if he was within earshot.

"My goodness, man." Tavov ran toward him. "What's the matter?" Mila followed on his heels. All three of them finally reached the front door step.

"The fields," R.J. called out. "There's a fire. Call for help. Now!"

"My crop," Tavov wailed as he ran out the door behind him. "It's on fire. The whole field will go up in minutes."

"Angel!" R.J. yelled out her name even as he prayed she wasn't in there. But his sixth sense told him otherwise. He heard a faint sob behind him and realized Mila had followed him to the edge of the field.

It was impossible to see more than a few feet into the fields. It appeared the flames had fully engulfed the center. If that was the case, and Angel was in there…

No! Not like this. God, he couldn't lose her. Especially not like this.

"Angel," he yelled louder. "Answer me!"

He quickly took off his jacket and shirt, subconsciously considering how flammable the material was.

"R.J.," Mila's despondent voice cried out to him. "What are you doing? It's no use."

He moved closer toward the fire.

"R.J., stop!" This time it was Tavov. "It's destroyed. There's nothing you can do. Where are you going?"

"Just stay back," R.J. ordered and turned to make sure they had obeyed.

There was no time to explain. Besides, they would try to stop him. After all, he had no clear proof that she was in there. But his gut told him she was. And for now, that was all he needed.

He choked as clouds of black smoke hit his lungs. He'd had to escape and jump from blasts before. But he'd never actually been inside a fire. What if he failed?

His father's voice chose that moment to ram through his panicked brain.

"You're too big for your britches, boy. Sooner or later you're gonna fail. You think you're good enough to do anything. You're not."

He had to be. He had to be good enough for this. He had to get her out of there. Or die trying.

"Angel!" He looked around, his vision almost

completely obstructed now. The hairs on his skin started to singe. He was running out of time. What if she was on the other side of the field? There were rows and rows of plants. She could be anywhere.

And then he knew. Or he hoped he knew. He ran to the other side of the field. He had precious little time.

Please, let her have gone there.

He was only a few feet from the spot where they had both struggled to unearth the one plant. The same spot where he'd given in to the urge to finally touch her. Where she'd made him laugh as she shuddered in fear and disgust at the many bugs he was making her sit in.

He wasn't the kind of man someone like her deserved.

Or so he had thought. Now, with death staring him in the face, he almost laughed at that. It was up to him to become that man, and for her, he would.

If only he found her in time. He'd tell her all that. He'd tell her everything.

CHAPTER FOURTEEN

ANGEL TRIED TO curb the panic surging through her. She had to think. Rapid tears ran down her face. Flames danced around her, courting her like a demonic partner. She wasn't afraid of dying. At least she didn't think so. She was afraid of the agonizing pain.

Could a person willingly force herself into a catatonic state? She was out of options here.

Options. Choices. Choices she'd had, and the paths she'd chosen. All of it flashed before her eyes in an instant. She felt a sob emerge through her as she gagged. If she'd have the chance to do it over again, she'd do it so much differently. She loved him. And he loved her. She would make him see that. Somehow she'd make him understand.

If given the chance, she'd show him he meant more to her than anything else. Definitely more than returning to her life as Richard Scott's daughter and sole heir.

She choked out another sob as the thick smoke

burned through her sinuses and throat. Consciousness slowly edged away, and she welcomed the comfort of darkness.

She could almost hear him. Could almost hear his voice calling out to her. But she knew it was a dream. Knew it was too late.

She managed to utter his name. And then the darkness started to press heavier and heavier. She felt the hard ground beneath her and realized she didn't remember falling.

Coughing. Someone was coughing. Was it her? It was just so hard to try to concentrate.

Suddenly, miraculously, she felt herself lifted. Someone was here. Someone was helping her.

She could only pray she wasn't imagining it.

The burning light was different this time. She could still taste the smoke in the back of her throat, but it didn't burn as strongly. Angel fought to open her eyes, not sure if she really wanted to.

This light *was* different. It was coming from a lamp above her.

Did heaven have lamps?

"Well, look who's finally stirring."

And apparently heaven had greeters who sounded just like Shanna.

Angeline tried to speak, but dryness stilled her tongue. "W-water…"

Someone touched plastic to her lip, and she opened her mouth as cool, smooth liquid slid down her throat. It hurt like hell to swallow. She forced herself to open her eyes completely, slowly letting the brightness seep in.

A familiar face hovered above her. She felt a smile form on her lips.

"N-not heaven," she croaked out.

"Well, I'm not sure how to take that comment."

Angel felt a comforting hand gently take hold of her wrist.

"Shan."

"Shh…" the other woman cooed. "I'm here, darling. I'm right here. But you take it easy, okay?"

"'Kay…"

"More water?"

Angel tried to nod but only managed a slight lift of her head. The plastic touched her lips again, and she sipped from it slowly. Exhausted from the small effort, she sank her head deeper into the pillow.

"Alive," Angel muttered, more to seek validation of her unexpected state.

Shanna nodded above her. "Yes, darling. You're alive. And you're going to be fine."

"S-sorry."

"Well, you should be." Shanna's voice broke. "I distinctly told you when you left not to play with fire."

Angeline did her best impression of a laugh. "Y-you m-meant R—" She stopped. It took several moments before she could resume. "R.J." She finally managed to finish.

Shanna nodded. "Yes, yes, of course." She then turned and left the room.

Angeline felt too tired to try to figure out why Shanna had left. And the burning sensation in her eyes was intensifying. Closing her lids slowly, she allowed herself to drift back to sleep, not even hearing the excited voices of the three people when they entered the room.

"You know they're going to start charging you rent here if you don't wake up soon." R.J. tried to sound casual as Angel slowly roused herself from sleep. As jokes went, it was a pretty lame one. And her startled eyes told him she hadn't really heard it.

She tried to sit up, and he immediately reached to help her. "Whoa, there. Take it easy."

"What are you doing here?" She spoke very slowly, and he felt his chest tighten at the thought of all the pain she must be in. He sat on the edge of the bed near her pillow and gently took her into his arms.

"We've been waiting for you to wake up again. Who knew it was going to take you another whole day?"

"We?"

"Yeah, Shanna's here, too. And my business partner, Tom. He flew her personally in the jet when they heard what had happened."

"You flew back?" she asked him.

"He never left," Shanna's voice boomed cheerily from the doorway.

Angel's confusion showed on her face. Shanna moved closer to the bed.

"How are you?" Shanna reached for Angeline's hand and sat beside him on the side of the bed.

"I—I guess I'm fine."

Angel turned questioning eyes back to him. He trailed a finger down her cheek. He had to touch her. To make sure she was really there. "I came back to talk to you. One more time, I figured, before I left for the States. I saw the fields on fire and realized you must have been in there."

"B-but how?"

R.J. shrugged.

"Isn't it just like a man?" Shanna gave him a mocking glare. "Leaving out the best details. He just knew, Angeline. And he managed to find you. Luckily, by then you'd managed to get yourself far enough away from the smoke."

R.J. watched as Angeline's mouth came open. "You saved me?"

He touched a finger to her lips. He didn't need or want words of gratitude. She'd never understand fully that he'd jump into hundreds of fires for her if he had to.

She acknowledged the gesture with a slight movement of her head. "What happened? How did it start?"

R.J.'s arms tightened around her. "No one really knows. Probably one of the celebratory candles from the wedding made its way to the field. Or someone dropped a cigar that smoldered until it finally caught flame."

Her lips tightened. "Is everyone okay?"

"You were the only one near the fields. No one

else was injured. And the doctor Mila and Tavov had check you out said you were very lucky."

She dropped her gaze, and he could anticipate her next question.

"The crop?"

He'd been right.

He tightened his lips, not wanting to dump the bad news on her. But she was going to find out sooner or later. "I'm sorry," he replied finally.

"All of it?"

"I'm afraid every last plant was destroyed before they could put the fire out."

She shut her eyes tight. "H-how are Mila and Tavov taking it?"

"They're just glad no one was hurt," he tried to reassure her.

He could see her desperate effort to try to compose herself as she processed the news. "There isn't even one bush left? Nothing with which they can replant from?" she asked, her voice shaky.

He blew out a deep breath. "Angel, don't do this to yourself."

"Please, R.J. I need to know. Is there any possibility something was salvaged?"

He rubbed his face and stood. "I'm afraid not,

sweetheart. The fire destroyed every single plant on the Bays' property."

Desolation filled her eyes, and he could do nothing but give her the full finality of it. "The Bays told me there's nowhere else it can be found. It only grows on this soil. And every last plant is gone."

Her reaction to this last bit of news confused the hell out of him. Her eyes grew wide, but not with sadness this time. Then a slow smile spread across her face. He watched in shock as the grin turned into all-out laughter. He decided to ring for the doctor when her laughter grew even louder.

"No, no. I'm okay. I think things may turn out okay, after all." R.J.'s look told her he clearly thought she'd lost it.

"Angel, I just told you that the Bays lost every single last plant."

She smiled again. "Maybe not," she said. "Maybe not."

"It's wonderful to see you up and about again, dear." Mila stood from where she was kneeling and brushed the dirt off her knees.

"How's the soil prep going?"

"Fine, fine. Luckily, the ground was moist

enough that it wasn't damaged too deeply. And thank the heavens you had that plant in your room. I shudder to think what we'd have lost if you hadn't had the impulse to want one in your room. With the way Mila's Bloom divides and spreads, we might have a small harvest within a couple of seasons. Not much, but that will change with time." She gave her a wide smile. "That would certainly make your product much more exclusive initially."

Then Mila scanned Angeline with concerned eyes. "But enough about that. How are you feeling? Will you be able to make your trip tomorrow?"

"I think so. It's R.J.'s company's private plane. I'll have the three of them to take care of me."

As if on cue, Tom and Shanna materialized out of the fields. Shan had streaks of dirt around her cheeks and nose. Tom was fast on her heels. They both looked annoyed.

"Look, stop pestering me. I don't need your help," Shanna was insisting.

"Why are you so damn stubborn? All I did was carry some lousy water for you."

They stormed right past Angeline and Mila as Shanna replied in a huff, "You're the stubborn one. Even though I said not to, you yanked those buckets right out of my hands. If you're planning to play hero, forget it. Been there, done that." She threw her hands in the air.

Angeline watched them descend toward the house and turned to give Mila an inquisitive look.

"They've been acting like that since they got here," the older woman said.

Angel smiled. "Looks like it's going to be an interesting flight." Her attention returned to the matter at hand, and the heavy weight once again settled inside her chest.

"Mila, I—I need to discuss something with you and Tavov before we leave. I meant to do this before—" she paused and let out a breath "—before everything happened."

"Tavov had to go purchase some materials. Why don't the two of us talk until he gets here?"

Angel started chewing her bottom lip. "I was kind of hoping to tell you both at once."

Mila reached and took her hand. She started leading her to the wooden park bench a few feet away.

"I think it might be better if us girls chatted a little bit first," Mila insisted.

Angel sat down on the bench with a thud, then

shifted uncomfortably as her thighs hit the hard surface. She hadn't suffered any serious burns, but her skin was still tender. It was like she'd fallen asleep under the sun.

For several hours, near the equator, in the nude.

She shook her head and berated herself for the negative thoughts. She'd been very lucky.

"All right, then," she began. "What I'm about to say isn't going to be easy."

Mila gave her an understanding look. It was enough encouragement to just spill it all out.

"Mila," she started again, "the ugly truth is that R.J. and I weren't really together when I told you we were. I mean, at first we were. We were originally, but when we told you that we were, we weren't."

Mila's expression didn't change. "I mean," Angel tried to continue, realizing she wasn't making any sense, "we were, but we were officially separated."

God, this was harder than she had thought. "We lied, Mila. I lied, so that Tavov would at least start negotiating. R.J. was just trying to help me. Then we were going to tell you, but I never mustered up enough courage to do it." She was rambling. She thumped her palm to her forehead. "I'm not making any sense, am I?" She must not be because Mila wouldn't still be sitting there so calmly if she was.

"Let me try this again." She turned to face the other woman, then felt a reassuring squeeze on her hand.

"It's all right dear, I think I understand."

"No, you can't really…"

"Angeline, dear, I do. I know all about it. I've known for a while now."

Angel blinked. Once, twice. Mila's hand patted hers. "But you never said anything."

"I felt you needed to tell me yourself. After you and R.J. had worked out your—how do you Americans say it? Issues? Hmm?"

"How long have you known?"

"I wasn't sure until the morning after the wedding."

"What gave us away?"

"You mean besides the longing that was so apparent in each of you? I could see that both of you were keeping yourselves at a distance. But the looks you stole when you thought the other wasn't looking… The real giveaway was your argument on the balcony that morning. Tavov and I were right below. We heard most of it."

Angel put a hand through her hair and looked out at the sea. "Oh my God, Tavov heard it, too?"

"He and I spoke about it. We both agreed to let you two settle it between yourselves before having to deal with us. Then it appeared you'd never get a chance when R.J. announced he was leaving. We also agreed that you hadn't actually ever lied to us. You were a married woman. And you both admitted to having problems that morning in Boston when I stopped by to check on you."

She'd never thought of it that way. Mila's words served as a figurative balm on her guilty soul. Much like the one she had to apply every few hours on her abused skin.

"Still, we should have told you that we knew. Please, please forgive us," Mila pled and squeezed her hand.

Now, that was irony. Mila was asking for forgiveness from *her*. The heavy weight on her heart finally lifted. "Only if you return the favor."

"It's hard to believe we've only been living in this suite for a week." Angeline stared out at the view from the balcony and felt R.J.'s hands on her upper arms.

"Something tells me you're ready to leave." She

allowed herself to lean back into him. He felt so solid, so secure.

"I wanted to come out here one last time." She turned to face him.

She rested her cheek against his chest. Still unable to believe he was here with her, holding her.

The avalanche of emotions running through her were hard to put into words. But she had to try. "We've been given another chance. I'd like to take it. A lot of things went wrong with us, R.J. But there's so much more that's so right. We need to look at *our* lives together, moving forward. Our future together is what matters now. Not what the past was, not what anyone else thinks."

He pulled her tighter against him and stroked her cheek with gentle fingers. "I know, sweetheart. Life is too precious to live it without you. I'm tired of going through the motions. I don't plan on making the same mistakes again."

A comfortable silence ensued, and she took advantage of it to merely savor the feel of his arms around her.

He rubbed his chin against the top of her head as he spoke. "And you don't have to worry about keeping TeaLC solvent until the next full harvest. I already have my finance people working on transferring the funds."

She stepped back to stare at him. "I don't want you to—"

He cut her off. "I am technically your partner, Angel. In every sense now. Let me invest in my own company." He smiled, then corrected, "Our company, that is."

"Thank you." It was all she could think to say, the emotion welling inside her close to choking her up.

"You're welcome." He gave her one last squeeze. "We better get going. I know TeaLC has been missing its leader for quite a while."

She slowly pulled out of his embrace to look at him. "That will take care of itself when Shanna gets back."

He lifted an eyebrow. "I don't understand."

"I've turned over the reins to its new CEO. Shanna deserves it. She knows the business as well as I do. She's already got the plans drawn for the launch of the newest product once the harvest is ready—Angel's Brew."

He smiled wide. "She's a genius."

"Besides, I'm much better at launch and development than I am at maintenance management."

He narrowed his eyes. "What exactly does that mean?"

"I'll be too busy to manage TeaLC."

"Busy doing what?"

"Focusing on what I'm good at." She touched a hand to his cheek. "And working on what I haven't been so good at in the past."

"Meaning?"

"I'm going to try to take TeaLC Works national." She'd come to the decision last night, surprised it hadn't occurred to her before. "To pitch the idea to other major corporations. I can show them exactly how to recruit from women's shelters and how much of a philanthropic effect it can have on the community.

"And if you let me, while I'm doing that, I'd like to work on being your wife."

As her answer, she felt herself being picked up and thoroughly kissed.

"Is that a yes?"

"I think it's about time we had a real honeymoon," he said with a laugh.

"You mean you'd actually be willing to risk another trip with me?"

He set her down and rubbed his jaw. "Mmm, maybe not. We don't actually have to go anywhere. It's really not necessary. Especially given what I want to do for most of our honeymoon."

"And what would that be?" she asked before realizing what a loaded question it was.

He gave her a wicked wink, and she had to laugh. "But aside from that." He cleared his throat, and his eyes suddenly turned serious. Slowly, she let him take her in his arms and hold her close.

"I just want to hold you. I just want to dance."

She tilted her head to look up at him, the surge of emotion almost too much for her heart to handle. "We get in trouble when we dance together. You said so yourself."

"Mmm-hmm," he agreed. "I know. Why don't we start now?"

* * * * *

If you enjoyed this book, don't miss
MISS PRIM AND THE
MAVERICK MILLIONAIRE,
the debut novel by Nina Singh. Available now!

If you can't wait to read
another fake relationship
romance then make sure you treat yourself to
THE MILLIONAIRE'S REDEMPTION
by Therese Beharrie.

MILLS & BOON®
Large Print – November 2017

The Pregnant Kavakos Bride
Sharon Kendrick

The Billionaire's Secret Princess
Caitlin Crews

Sicilian's Baby of Shame
Carol Marinelli

The Secret Kept from the Greek
Susan Stephens

A Ring to Secure His Crown
Kim Lawrence

Wedding Night with Her Enemy
Melanie Milburne

Salazar's One-Night Heir
Jennifer Hayward

The Mysterious Italian Houseguest
Scarlet Wilson

Bound to Her Greek Billionaire
Rebecca Winters

Their Baby Surprise
Katrina Cudmore

The Marriage of Inconvenience
Nina Singh

1017 Rom LP

MILLS & BOON®
Large Print – November 2017

An Heir Made in the Marriage Bed
Anne Mather

The Prince's Stolen Virgin
Maisey Yates

Protecting His Defiant Innocent
Michelle Smart

Pregnant at Acosta's Demand
Maya Blake

The Secret He Must Claim
Chantelle Shaw

Carrying the Spaniard's Child
Jennie Lucas

A Ring for the Greek's Baby
Melanie Milburne

The Runaway Bride and the Billionaire
Kate Hardy

The Boss's Fake Fiancée
Susan Meier

The Millionaire's Redemption
Therese Beharrie

Captivated by the Enigmatic Tycoon
Bella Bucannon

MILLS & BOON®

Why shop at millsandboon.co.uk?

Each year, thousands of romance readers find their perfect read at millsandboon.co.uk. That's because we're passionate about bringing you the very best romantic fiction. Here are some of the advantages of shopping at www.millsandboon.co.uk:

* **Get new books first**—you'll be able to buy your favourite books one month before they hit the shops

* **Get exclusive discounts**—you'll also be able to buy our specially created monthly collections, with up to 50% off the RRP

* **Find your favourite authors**—latest news, interviews and new releases for all your favourite authors and series on our website, plus ideas for what to try next

* **Join in**—once you've bought your favourite books, don't forget to register with us to rate, review and join in the discussions

Visit **www.millsandboon.co.uk**
for all this and more today!